GELATIN SILVER PRINT

GELATIN SILVER PRINT

TIGE LEWIS
QUINTINA

Copyright © 2008 by Tige Lewis Quintina.

Library of Congress Control Number: 2008902021
ISBN: Hardcover   978-1-4363-2706-0
                Softcover   978-1-4363-2705-3

All rights reserved. No part of this book may be reproduced or transmitted in any form or by any means, electronic or mechanical, including photocopying, recording, or by any information storage and retrieval system, without permission in writing from the copyright owner.

This book is a work of fiction. Names, characters, places, and incidents either are products of the author's imagination or are used fictitiously. Any resemblance to actual events or locales or persons, living or dead, is entirely coincidental.

Copyedited by Sheila May O. Cartoneros
Reviewed by Charisse M. Desabelle

This book was printed in the United States of America.

To order additional copies of this book, contact:
Xlibris Corporation
1-888-795-4274
www.Xlibris.com
Orders@Xlibris.com
46170

CONTENTS

I.	Prologue	17
II.	The Tides	25
III.	Summertime	36
IV.	When We Were Gods	37
V.	A Sonnet For The Lost	49
VI.	With Zane At The Town Line	50
VII.	An Aperitif With Madam Fate	59
VIII.	Buildings Like Doll Houses	67
IX.	At San Sebastiano In Mantua	71
X.	The Woman In Room 29	72
XI.	The Sighs Of The Sun	84
XII.	The Waste Land	87
XIII.	An Ode To Audrey Wilde	96
XIV.	The Siamese Fighting Fish	97
XV.	The Lights Of The City	107
XVI.	At The Mad Fish	108
XVII.	One January Night	113
XVIII.	At The Tamarack	114
XIX.	The Lady With The Dog	122
XX.	The Doors On The Street	123
XXI.	A Lullaby To Vanity	128

For Juliana

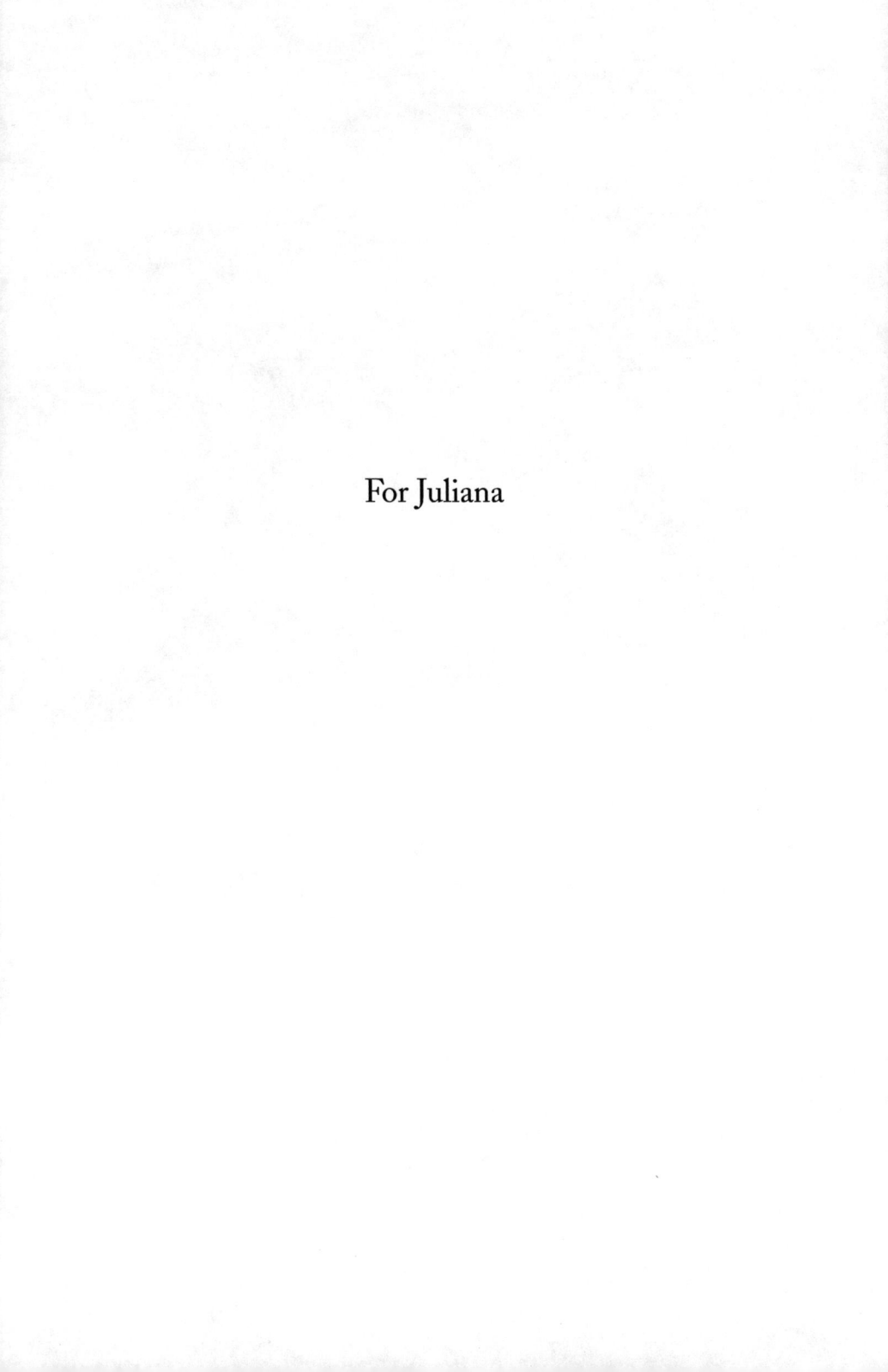

'A guest', I answer'd, 'worthy to be here.'
    Love said, 'You shall be he.'
'I, the unkind, the ungrateful? Ah, my dear,
    I cannot look on thee.'
Love took my hand and smiling did reply,
    'Who made the eyes but I?'

        —George Herbert, "Love"

We are not sure of sorrow,
    And joy was never sure;
To-day will die to-morrow;
    Time stoops to no man's lure;
And love, grown faint and fretful,
    With lips but half regretful
Sighs, and with eyes forgetful
    Weeps that no loves endure.

—Algernon Charles Swinburne,
    "The Garden of Proserpine"

Muses, lovers of the arts, daughters of Zeus and Mnemosyne, hear me in this request to you, bright and unbound . . . speak . . . and begin this story . . .

FOREWORD

If one is interested in further elucidating the book, many sources have influenced its narratives and symbols. The first and plainest is the title Gelatin Silver Print, which anyone familiar with the art of photography will immediately recognize. Also inspirational to the idea were visits to the collections at the Museum of Fine Arts in Boston, Massachusetts, during the late 1990s. I recommend the essay on Photography by Marc Scheps, "The Art of Photography," presented in Benedikt Taschen Verlag's 1996 book, 20th Century Photography, Museum Ludwig Cologne.

One could further study the cinematic montages of Russian filmmaker Lev Kuleshov and the work of Soviet film director and theorist Sergei Mikhailovich Eisenstein. I suggest investigating the Kuleshov Effect by viewing Lev Kuleshov's experimental short film using the face of Ivan Mozzhukhin. For this manuscript, instead of a darkened cinema and a strip of celluloid rolling at twenty-four frames per second, written stories and poetry are juxtaposed.

The Waste Land and *The Love Song of J. Alfred Prufrock* by Thomas Sterns Eliot also greatly influenced this manuscript. Other works of influence are *Candide* or *Optimism* by Francois-Marie Arouet De Voltaire (the translation from French I chose was of Robert M. Adams). The works of F. Scott Fitzgerald, especially, *This Side of Paradise* and *The Great Gatsby*; Homer's, *Iliad* and *Odyssey* (the translations from Greek I chose were of Robert Fitzgerald's); and the writings of Ernest Hemingway, especially his *A Farewell to Arms* and *The Old Man and the Sea*. Anyone familiar with these will immediately recognize a strong homage.

ACKNOWLEDGMENTS

This would not have been possible without Juliana. She is an incredibly strong woman, a terrific parent to Eric, and my best friend. She shows me every day what all the songs and poems on love were written about. She is a great person.

My parents, Pryce and Donna, have always been my biggest supporters. Very special thanks to my mother for inspiring me to be a good man and to think and read and write. Very special thanks to my father for his love, strength, and support.

My siblings, Brent, Laura, and Pryce, teach me all the time life is about having fun, sticking together, and not sweating the small stuff.

Specific thanks must go to the following that helped make this book possible: Peter Filonowicz, Liza Ableson, Ron DiBona, Rob and Surrey Elwell, Kathleen Haley, Sewel Hayes, Yegi Hong, Michael Hunt, Charles and Kathy Hunt, Mike Lane, Mark McManus, Elijah Newton, Loretta Ostmann, Billy Reinstein Jr., Geoffrey H. Richon, Karen Ristuben, Renee Scudder, Eastern Point Yacht Club, Emerson College, Harvard University, the Sunny Day Café, Dr. Peter A. and Katherine L. Coakley at Finnegan's Pub, Boston Fine Artist Aimée Lee Empey, and last but not least, the Right Honorable Lady of the Silent Green Forest, Rebecca Clements.

Cover photo by award winning photographer, Judith Monteferrante, *www.jmonteferrante.com*. Email at info@jmonteferrante.com. Studios in Westchester, NY and Gloucester, MA.

PROLOGUE

"There is nothing better for thee Athanasia, than to drink and find enjoyment in thy food." Ambrose Silenus—lumberjack, barrel-chested sophomore—walked his particular walk followed by an almost military posturing of shoulders, the effect smashed by the consumed half room of almost mocking light. He held a liter of whiskey and a purple plum. He had just chopped down the largest tree.

"Scott is in love. Our own Scott. Our own Scotty Theseus." Ambrose sat in plum chair and ate his plum and plumbed his juicy heart.

Myna Pallas Athene—wise woman of the arts, junior at Boston's Massachusetts College of Art—laughed her gray-eyed laugh. Ambrose was amusing.

"Vanity!" Ambrose continued. "Listen. Watch him primp! Can we hear her name again? Audrey! The wench! Audrey! Audrey! I drink to thee, merry Audrey, and for God's sake, Scotty, give me a copy of your book!"

Scott woke from daydreaming, thunderstorming, photo-filling bubbles in his head. His thoughts of school, professors, and books floated through the sultry air. He looked around Finnegan's bar and smiled at his pint of Guinness. College is for fools. A business designed to make money, not to teach. The best teaching comes from beer. Good beer.

Scott drank down his pint. Too early for lunch, too late for breakfast. Might as well drink. I've earned it. All As in school, all Fs in love. Too late to sleep and dream days again. Maybe I should pray. Let us pray for those—for them—the ones that passed. Maybe they can all be resurrected. With what? Tea always resurrects me. For what? What is the chief end of human life? To know God by whom men were created. What reason have I for saying so? Because it certainly is not love.

All things come and go and there's nothing anyone can do—Ezra Mann where are you? Nothing endures. It is entropy that does it—returns all to chaos. And we don't help fighting and destroying everything. What's next? Perhaps a War on Love. We've fought everything else. Why not? I wish I had a bomber loaded with champagne and roses. A suicide bombing on all poets and dreamers.

School is done. I quit. The day is fleeting fast. Every thesis completed except the one on *her*. Thesis. Antithesis. It must be finished. Without an end. One must have an end. "True love never dies." Actually, there is one more thesis. To win love back. Audrey wanted to marry money. She left because I was a philosopher. Call me Gatsby. Oh, love is a mean joke. Audrey was in love with money. She loved it hard and left because I did not love it too. I was in love with her. Great Zeus grant me victory just once. Ambrose mentions my book! It is Audrey's really. One big joke on her. I wrote it far above them all. An artist's book. A collection of photographs a gallery. And thank God for beer and for the rent that is not due.

"Ambrose, enough already, shut up! Shut up!" Scott yelled at Ambrose.

"Shut up!" Scott yelled at Ambrose.

"Drink your breakfast, lad!"

"Drink your grog bowl, you dog! Oh, and here is my bloody book!" Scott—august, decorously long and lanky, with his handsome lower jaw—threw the new book to the floor by Ambrose's feet.

"Final honors for the departed." Ambrose laughed, picking up the book. "Everyone dies, Scotty. That's the truth. We all are doomed. So forget death and live. It is no sweat on us. Just have fun. Eat, drink, be merry, and drink! Our honor student gets all As and then quits school and now regrets. You won't get her back by selling yourself out. That old love is dead too and does not grow in the sun. Comets at night gun for earth, and the stars weep—but for you, not for her. Your romance is what's gnawing you. You're too deep. That's what you get for having wits. Forget her and drink! Drink with me! Write another book, and forget medical school, forget women, forget love! And do not dishonor Finnegan's and Peter, our great host, by being glum!"

Scott crisped his eyes, seared his look toward Ambrose, rolling sands over sand. He ignored all but his own inner voice. The book had been out now a month, and Papa did not call. Not yet. Papa will not call. He never reads. Has any of the family read it? I sent out all the copies, one to each. No one cares perhaps. Telephones. Faxes. Morse code. Smoke signals. As a matter of security, the Department of Homeland Security had surveillance installed on all the wires. Pinky red green licorice wiretaps. Such a lovely and judicious piece, lights the fires by burning it. Wouldn't it be nice if the book caused that much stir?

Meanwhile, the politicians should be tied to a car fender and dragged. For every pothole in the street dragged one block. Chefs should be fed, and judges should be critiqued. Perhaps the book should be dragged with the politicians or, better yet, used to fill the gaps of the potholes. The roads are not smooth. The mayor spends money to fix local politics, but not the bloody roads. Dragged over the potholes, I say. That will keep everyone honest.

Asphalt roads. Lots of pavement. Shoestring pavement from Rockport to Gloucester. Boston to New York. New York to London has no road. Has anyone called? Apparently, I have no fans. Forget it and the other. Perhaps I am secretly dead. Wandering the River Styx—the newest living bearer of the dream. Yet where are the angels? To hell with the winged devils in their flight. To hell with the complications of the heart. Here's to life. A drink! Too bad I was not shot. Mankind cannot have such dreams amongst it. The first in command under dreams. Indivisible. For freedom and justice for all. Amen. Thou art Moses, and upon this rock I will build. Secrets in the sunshine. It will have a tombstone. My "happy heart." Here died the aorta. Bury the book in the earth, and Papa will leave flowers. Upon it, it shall read, "Here lies love. God made it an offer it couldn't refuse."

Thunderstorms. The spring morning is damn sticky. It's ninety-five today, and there's plenty of beer behind the bar. It's so cool in the bar called Finnegan's. Terrific air-conditioning. I wonder where Audrey is. I own nothing now. Not even those memories. Those long-faded prints have been washed each day with soda water. And each night, Hera takes a washcloth and, while I dream, dips it in the stardust and wipes my mind clean of it. My love. I can hardly remember. No sound, no voice. Is that mermaid's singing, each to each. Her singing like the siren call that smashed mariners upon the rocks. Yet in the sky, there sit her eyes: Pollux and Castor, cold and unblinking. I cannot see them now, but they are there. I wait for winter when they return.

I can smell the ocean and the sea in the sky. It would be nice to push the clouds like dust piles and sweep them away. Where is she? The hot sun beats, but I cannot see. If only they'd shoot a missile up to clear the clouds. Shake the dust. That would do it. Then we'd have a lover's day. A dust-free day. Gorgeous!

No more love. I quit. Not another loving thought. This heart is done. The world aches from that wound. What is it all for anyway? Each love is dead, either in matter or in spirit, and with each, killed off bits inside me too.

A life, ten thousand years old, casting white light and shadows on rooftops of sprinkled streets for the tourists to see. Maybe God forgot how it is to feel, so we must feel everything for it. August is a good month for good fishing. Good, plump, sweet fish. Unlike May. May rains. Wild rain. Silverfish. Shooting stars. That was three? No, it is a blasphemy. Audrey is the one who travels to the corners of our mind, through winding valleys of wrinkled rock, under that bright sun. Audrey Wilde.

"I'm going to order some eggs and pancakes with butter and maple syrup." Scott willed his arm toward Ambrose and reached for the phone.

"You see! Those were Scott's first, Scott's last: Scott, before he left; Scott, before he began; Scott, as he snapped off into the darkness—a broken film falling from the projector that birthed his illusory life. The Scott we have lost." Ambrose, the noble drunkard, bellowed and burped, grumbled and leaned and tossed the modern marvel. A three step to the chowder head that thing makes one. "He's got the tripod effect: needs it to feel whole. 'Who might love me?' Stop thinking about her!" Ambrose shouted. Scott was drowned in electrostatic microwaves.

Audrey liked to jump. To climb on things. She'd stop to rest. Her back firm and strong. She climbed hard. No one sees her climbing anymore. Did I dial? I remember you, Audrey. I remember thee, and I dial. Numbers set in stone. Stand on your large stone looking about, and from that, dream and deem it right. To hell with my book. Why do I write when instead I could be a capitalist? What if I could phone her? Would she say, "My darling Scott . . . Scott . . . dear Scott, all is well, and I love you. Thank you, darling. Now play the stock market please."

They were to deliver the bacon and pancakes. Scott threw down the phone and picked up that morning's paper. His Holiness is giving up on Tibet and moving into a condominium in Old Town Marblehead, Massachusetts? Why not? There's great sailing there and three anonymous meetings a day. Let us wish him well in his recovery. Don't pick on one religion. They, all of them, need to be twelve stepped. Not one lives up to his or her own creed of love thy neighbor.

I wish I could love my neighbor. She is a very pretty redhead named Michelle. I am sure I have dialed her in my sleep. She's just very shy. And why try? All love ends. Just sleep, and punch numbers in my sleeping head. The crickets string their crunchy violin legs to sleep. Perhaps this is the waste land. The king is ill. Everything is in despair.

Where is my breakfast? My eggs and pancakes? It's taking them long enough. I feel guilty eating eggs. Are they alive? No, not fertilized. They are far from any trimester. Semester. For her I dedicate the book: To Audrey, a plague on both our houses. Love. Loss. Lazy, cabal-ist-ic-ally crazy. Do we know enough to hate love? Life feeds on life, everything, plant and animal must eat to live. Yet only humans feed on love. The wasteland fills our sleep. A thousand repentances dissolve. Yes, she says and smiles. Audrey smiled happy through her angling nose and wrinkling blue eyes. She was a rose head on mahogany. Audrey is the currents of the colors in the woods; the flower and all its petals are her, swelled and big as the moon, swelled as eyes with tears juicy; and the fall of my chest empty—that is, the closed-middle, the hidden, the ambiguous mystery: Audrey.

"Do not forget your nicotine patch, you pirate!" Ambrose Silenus, chop-chip-chopping with bare hands, roared. "Twelve per day to make up for one night of lost love."

Traces of the past night's escapades with friends. Rejoinder. What a bore. Will we ever be the same? Can we move on in this new world and still have the same spirit? Planes have crashed into our buildings, people we love fight people who love other people who love still other people. The commercials, the apple pie, the baseball, all turn our world; and we forget. Some want everything. And why not? It is all about loss eventually, so why not gain? Much more to lose is more, isn't it?

"Change, ain't nothin' stays the same . . ." Myna sang Van Halen lyrics.

Scott lifted a bottle of Irish whiskey, refilling Myna's glass with liquid love.

"Is it morning?" Myna, the junior from Mass College of Art which Ambrose dubbed *'Le Art de Mass'* and looked around with tired eyes.

"Much past morning, Myna darling. Myna . . ." Ambrose waxed. "If only I had Aladdin's lamp, I would wish you a good painter so you could paint that green glass red. Give me a kiss, you villain, now that your breath is fresh with spirits!"

"I would if you had a cock and a set of jewels to kick in," Myna spoke, listening lazily to the Gershwin on the gramophone. That is no lie, Finnegan's has a gramophone.

"Such a lovely playing. Today I'm Ginger Rogers." Myna's gay voice sprang. "And I wish for Gene Kelly."

"Rodgers danced with Fred Astaire."

"Exactly."

"Gene Kelly." Ambrose Silenus snuffed. "Preposterous. Drink, there, Myna, you minx. Drink, you minxy Myna. You are a festival of wenches. You blue-blooded American wh . . . wait, I think we've lost Scott . . ." Ambrose Silenus shouted in a guttural criticism, "Scott! Why don't you marry minxy Myna over here? You like to dance! She likes to sing! *Martre* here wants love, don't you, minxy?"

Myna lay back in the large, plush green chair and rolled her gray eyes.

"He would make a good husband for you, minx. He can perform."

"You are my hero." Myna yawned at him.

Ambrose clapped.

"Look at Scott, he plays foosball by himself! Who do you play with, Scott? Juliet's ghost? The spirit of Audrey? Perhaps both?"

And that is that, is it not, Audrey? Shall we go? Let's start this, please! *Click . . . Click . . . Click . . . Click-click . . . Click-click-click . . . Click-click-click-click . . . Tat-tatat-atatata-tatatatataata-ataaataat-aaaaaaaaaataaa-aataaaaaaaaataaa . . .*

(A narrative begins in the field of time.)

"What about me for a husband, minx?" Ambrose Silenus, gunned with ammo made of rubber, marked the musing of Myna. She came with articulation.

"I'd rather marry Vomit."

"How could you refuse me!"

"I am much too much of an idealist for marriage, and even if I did give in to the romance of a situation, which you could never provide, I know it would be purely out of sentiment. In other words, I'd marry you for your money."

Ambrose stopped dead, pursed his wet lips wetting them more, more, and more—each juicy and waxed and rich.

"I'd make you a real woman."

"You'll nauseate me once a month thence."

Ambrose winked and fixed his doggish hair and sat up straight.

"I care about Scott too much to flog you through. Look at the poor louse. I could never forgive myself. You and your Scotty here are too easily drawn to the wrong ones, like moths to the spark. And what then if there's a sunbeam in the room? Do you capture it? Embrace? Hold on tight, right? The sun shifts, and then what? Following blindly the light to the sparks with your beating wings? Love is our only hope, you wenchy tart. Just like Scott, you fly to it. You cannot fool me! Forget Audrey, Scott! Forget the dead! Do your heart a favor. You savant! Run for president of the United States. Become an astronaut. Be a doctor. Fix it! Get your Nobel Prize! Bring love back to the world! If you lose your senses, we might all win, but do not claim winning is love! Moments are where they are at. Moments with momentous people. The rest is loss. That is why I like drinking and eating and the ocean and the sun. Who needs love when I got a full stomach, a glass of beer, and the waves lit up by a thousand golden suns?"

Myna drew a tissue from her purse, wiped her nose with it, and threw it at Ambrose's head.

"Whip your own slime with that. I do not want to hear you farting in your booze. You are making me sick and ruining this song and this whiskey!"

Ambrose sat back—elbows back, palms high, holding his head up straight—and relaxed with a sigh. The lumberjack spitted two spats in his palms, rubbed, and swung his axe.

"Something about that ocean reminds me of those lazy times when it is all swirling around, sharp and jazzy like confetti, incredibly subtle and unspoken, like the brilliant bursts in your blue eyes."

"My eyes are gray." Myna indicated with a sip of amber love, gargled, and spitted it into the paper cup spittoon.

"Gray! You blubbering dope! The ocean's blue! Get original! God, you're such a man! You wonder why I'm a virgin." Myna closed her eyes. "Insensitive brat, go off in your mother's milk. Mighty Zeus, and save me from these Greeks."

Ambrose held his glass up to the air. "Toast to Zeus, father of the gods and men, and to Scotty's new wife! No. No. He is too much of a man for you, but don't worry, he has married his ghosts already. That poor sot married Audrey in his heart that first day they met. Perhaps he just needs to fornicate a whore? Myna, care to help him out?"

"Sell your kidney for a rub!" Myna sat back, closing her eyes and crossing her legs. "Or better yet, go get tight in Tijuana."

"I hear the mermaids singing, Scotty, singing! Don't you hear! They sing to drown Pangaean men chasing voices in the wind. Forget your Audrey. She will live as will you. Be sure to fill your book with nude photographs. Like the ones on the Internet. See the raw oysters snapping before our eyes. Award winners.

Look! The favorites of dead old men. You cannot masturbate now without being reprimanded by every well-meaning quasi-intellectual! Scott! She is salivating! Our goddess! Scott! Stop loafing in the isles. You haven't quit anything; you have become an artist. Accept it! Stand and make your peace. Take it like a man!"

Scott walked behind the bar and took out the ingredients to make a cup of coffee. Peter, Finnegan's proprietor, had set out a lovely pot of black Columbian beans. The aroma filled the air. It was a strong, dark brew. Nothing mixes better with black coffee than Guinness. It was the brilliant man's mimosa.

And what of this goddess? Is she Veronese? No, she is Greek. Some wisdom. I am wise. I make a choice between coffee and tea.

"Coffee or tea?" Scott asked.

"Whiskey." Ambrose bowed.

"Only drunks have whiskey for breakfast."

"Drunks and kings."

"Tea then?"

"If I were king, a sovereign, I would not be American. If I were a queen, I would be a real man, yet give me coffee. I hate tea. For its tea, then taxes. Whiskey and coffee, I'll take both. I'll take the tea and throw it in the sea, and then we can have another party and tax the English when they take their coffee at the four."

Scott made a mental note to sober up. Living as an artist is hard when you are drunk.

"Scott's constantly making mental notes now that he's an artist. I can read it in your eyes better than on this book! And what about a game? Shall we play Farkle? Or do you feel like losing at foosball? What will you do when your lineage learns of your lack of mental luster? Raise our taxes? Like a large journal, his brain is only bigger, but only understandable to those who have drowned. Or married, I should say."

Scott endured a few sips of the hot coffee.

"Must I stay drunk for an entire day? You have not stopped for two nights! Just because you are rich, got your trust fund. Get on then to the next. You are married to an annuity. You can go live the dream. Hang out with Paris Hilton and winter in Key Largo. You rich, think you own the world. You may inherit it, but you do not own it. You'll lose everything like all the rest. There's no taking it with you, after all. Try wearing that thought with your dunce cap. Don't ever let him influence you, Myna, this Lord of Dunces. When has he given any of that cash he fell into toward anything but his own fancy? He'll have you hunting pigs with him when we should be building a fire. Take your ambrosia, hire yourself a philosopher. Better yet, Ambrose, get a haircut and dry up! Take twelve steps off the nearest bridge, two aspirin, and one cup arsenic and do not skip the soda. Now get your feet off Peter's bar!"

"Can you believe the way our artist speaks?" Ambrose ran a bear paw through the head of fuzzy bear hair. "Pay attention, Scott, and learn something!" Ambrose

Silenus removed his feet then replaced them. "And be sure to reprimand those close friends—democracy and liberty. Did you hear? Your Audrey left a message on that infernal cell phone—she did, she sounds a conspiring anarchist, she does. A *pinion*! 'Good morning and happy Friday,' her voice, all dainty like. 'I hope you had a good week.' Rather! 'I had an insane week at work,' she continues. 'Blah, blah, I had to sneak up to the roof to send you a note before the day was over. Check your email, I hope you have a good day, and take care.'"

"That's a very old message," Scott lamented. "Ancient. I haven't the heart to delete it."

"Old? But it was her! Your relegation."

"She called, yes. Long ago. Don't you get it?"

"Blimey, the fool! Did you hear that, Myna?"

"Who's the fool? You?" Myna yawned and lay back in the fluffy puffy chair. Fluffy puffy. Puffy fluffy. Ambrose stared, astonished and present.

"God, woman! Have not you been listening? Wisest of the wise, what is it that the bloody drugs have done to your mind? Marijuana, cocaine, crystal meth. You are a *Krista* now, you hyperbeauty?"

"Forget, you ass. I don't do drugs. Drugs are for losers like yourself. I exist for music and wisdom and art and fighting. And I, unlike you, contribute to this world. You, however, exist for your own amusement." Beams of sunny morning truth bounced behind her sleepless teeth.

"Forget that, Myna, I thought you knew! I am an ass! I am whole and through. For it is too late for me. You qualify to judge since you are femininity incarnate. Yes. From the beginning. Have you read Scott's book?"

"No."

"No? Why not?"

"I don't know. And stop shouting, fool!"

"Who's the fool? It is all in here! In this, our Scotty's book! You want to hear?"

He opened the book to page 1, then a brilliant flash and the bellow of hot air! The dusty floor swirled, and the reek of powder stirred.

"Scotty is Odysseus incarnate. Do not fear. The gods bless him. He has great Zeus' ear."

Myna swished her lavender-scented breath.

"Pay attention, harlot minx! The book begins when Scott was but a child!"

Myna fed scrambled eggs to the gray owl perched beside her and closed her gray-goddess eyes, and she listened.

THE TIDES

Scott Theseus surveyed the beach from the top of the small path. The day was hot. The ocean cheered with a slow roll of foam; and the sun, high in a bright blue sky, was all of everything. A group of tanned teenagers played Frisbee in the sand. Near them, a group of young children dug holes with plastic shovels, building walls for a castle. All over the beach, small groups of people buzzed with activity. Some people stood, squatting and talking; others sat on chairs, eating and laughing, or lying while watching the water or sleeping on great towels under the sun. The beach was overgrown with great colorful umbrellas with the long white poles that sprung from the sand like thin trunks of shiny trees. Everywhere, there was a celebration of the summer, the ocean, and the relaxation of it, of friendships, and of life.

Scott squinted and watched a sailboat inching by far off in the distance, its white sails full and sharp. The sun flashing platinum on the face of the sea—gold then white; the blue-green skin pushing to crests of rolling white foam, then sloping and falling with a sway up then draining out to a clear reflection of the sky. As Scott stood watching the water, a small bright purple ball flew over his head and landed on a blond woman near him. Scott heard the ball hit her and then her voice. He looked. He knew it was his football. He looked back and saw his brother, Avery, blushing, trying to hide.

"I wasn't ready!" Scott shouted. "That was your fault! I wasn't ready."

"You didn't catch it!" Avery yelled. Looking for an escape from the situation, he stood up on tiptoes. The blond woman had sat up. Scott looked at his brother and shook his head, yelling again. He looked at the woman and ran over to get his ball.

The blond woman wore a silver bathing suit and looked like the moon shimmering there in the summer heat. The sun reflected off a diamond from the button of her shiny brown belly. Scott wondered at her, believing anyone so pretty had to be famous and on television. The woman smiled at Scott.

"Sorry," he said.

"Watch it, you little bastard," she said, handing Scott the bright purple ball and lying back down. Scott apologized taking the ball, walking backward; then he turned and ran to his brother. Avery came down from his tiptoes.

"That was your fault, spaz," Scott condemned.

Avery shrugged.

"Where is Dad?"

Avery pointed.

Scott tossed the ball to Avery then ran toward his father who was walking toward them. He was easy to spot on the beach. Scott's father had an odd and funny walk. It was very unusual, and everyone who knew him could recognize him by it. The walk itself did its job, propelling him forward, but there was something very strange about it in the feet. It was a wide step, angled and outward, sort of thrusting dance move of each leg. Then there was the swinging of the arms. It was aerodynamic, though until you walked next to him you would not think so. He could move with great speed. Everyone remarked about it, but none thought lesser of Scott's father for it. Scott loved the walk because his father was very easy to spot in a crowd. His father, as usual, had begun setting up their camp.

"Come on." Scott motioned to Avery. The boys ran down the beach. Nearby, Scott spotted a group of old men on wooden beach chairs with a large red cooler between them. It served as a table of sorts for a chessboard, and they angled themselves around it as if in a living room at night. The chessboard was ornate, with artistically carved pieces made of white-and-black stone. The old men were watching the board, silent and thinking, sucking on large tobacco pipes. Scott stopped and watched. One old man who had a long white beard that fell past his belly sat chewing his pipe, blew a smoke ring, and then as if satisfied, smiled and moved a white piece and removed a black piece from the board. Another man with wild gray hair that stood straight up and crazy rubbed his chin and, with a big suck of smoke, bit his pipe while he thought. Scott saw three older women, wet from swimming, walk over to the men. They were glimmering with water beads and talking about iced peppermint tea. The tea sounded funny to Scott. He thought about how it would taste and then noticed Avery was not with him. He looked and found him with his father.

Scott's father had set up beach camp around a dull blue cooler, small radio, and three green-and-white chairs. Scott's shoes and his towel were laid out, and when he arrived, his father commenced to paint his skin with sunscreen. Scott liked the smell of it and always thought of the beach when he smelled it, even years after, when he long since grown up.

"Stand still." his father ordered, squirting the tannic white sunscreen on his hands and thrusting at Scott's face. Scott stood motionless and screwed his eyes tight shut. He heard the surf rolling and the voices of lifeguards in their orange suits talking words he could not follow. He wished he had an orange swimsuit, thinking of his green one, and remembered when he was younger and he could wear his underwear to the beach.

"Wipe that in," Scott's father commanded.

Scott proceeded to smear the tanning lotion all over, rubbing his face briskly, then his shoulders. He felt his father's strong hands on his back. When it was his brother's turn, Scott watched as Avery go rigid, giggling with his eyes squinted shut, his legs dancing from a perch on tiptoes. Those legs ran him away before his father could finish.

"Stand still, I said! Hey! You guys hungry?" his father asked, putting the tanning lotion down and sitting. He took off his sneakers, hid his car keys and money clip in the left one, then pushed a sock in after it. Scott watched. He did the same with his shoes. He placed three dollars into his shoe then pressed his sock in. Scott looked through the sandwiches in the cooler. As he did, a group of young girls, about eight or nine, walked by. He smiled and blushed. They ignored him. Just then, he remembered something he heard at school. He asked his father, "Dad, do crabs kiss?"

"What?"

"My friend Ezra told me if you hold two crabs together, they kiss."

"What? Eat that one." He handed Scott a sandwich. "It's tuna fish."

"Can I go crabbing today?" Scott asked.

"Stay with your brother. You want to go swimming?"

"Can I go snorkeling?"

"Stay away from the rocks. Make sure you come back after for more sunscreen, or you could sun burn."

Scott sat and ate his sandwich. When he was done, he grabbed his mask, snorkel, and fins. Avery grabbed his too. It frustrated Scott to see Avery with the same mask and fins. Avery was two years younger, and Scott had tried to explain Avery's being younger to his father when he was buying him the gear. Scott explained about Cousteau and diving, but it did no good. His father always bought two of everything.

Scott jumped on the sand toward the water and dreamed he could fly. He watched the gulls flying over the water and the sand diving, and he imagined if the model fighter planes he played with at Ezra's house were real.

That one P-51 Mustang, the Japanese Zero, and the F6F Hellcat, he remembered them all. He would fly away from everything, meet Jacques Cousteau and be the first person to dive with the Loch Ness monster and steer a submarine and work on the *Calypso*.

Some kids with brown wooden planks surfing the shallows caught his attention. Nearby, a few younger boys dug the sand into a small castle. The castle was circular and tall, and Scott inspected it from where he was. They should build a moat to move the first waters and construct an inside wall to protect the tower.

"Scotty, stay with your brother!" his father shouted.

Scott stood with his gear in hand and ran into the water's edge. He splashed through the water, cold and spilling over then seeping into the wet sand. He stood for a moment, adjusting his feet to the cold, then sat down in the shallows and attended to his gear.

The fins' hard strap hurt the back of his foot. But in the water, after adjustments, it slid on easy and felt all right. Scott looked back for Avery who was in the dry sand and, with the fins on his feet, was trying to walk, stomping his heels down and lifting his knees high, scooping sand and wobbling like a clown. Scott laughed.

"Spit in your mask," Scott instructed as he spit in his own mask.

"I know," said Avery.

"Spit and then rinse it."

"I know."

"Rinse it."

"I know," said Avery.

Scott put the mask on and stood backward into the waves. He set his snorkel properly and, when waist deep, turned and lay down, thrusting his face under the water. The waves were strong, and the cold water made Scott's lungs draw deep breath. A large wave crashed over and filled his snorkel. Scott stood, choking.

Avery was afraid to breathe through the snorkel; so he was crawling on his hands and knees, holding his nose, submerging his head, then lifting it out. Scott exhaled to clear the water from his snorkel then performed another big exhale, took the mask off, rinsed it, spitted in it, rinsed it again, and pulled the tight rubber strap over his head. The mask fit snuggly but leaked water near his nose; and after a few adjustments, the leak stopped, and he was able to submerge.

There was little sediment in the water, and Scott could see very clearly. He explored the bottom, touching the sand, shells, and bits of seaweed. He imagined barracuda and manta rays and eels and shot at them with an imaginary spear gun. He swam after a small orange crab, making a desperate grab for it, but went too deep; and water filled the snorkel with a rush that made Scott stand choking.

Thin clouds crept by the noon sun. Scott swam and played with his brother. Soon, they were joined by their father. He enjoyed swimming and playing in the water. He swam after them and grabbed at their legs, pretending he was a shark. He screamed and swam up beside Scott, took him by the hips and lifted and tossed him, splashing him into the waves. He held his hands so Avery could climb up—fins and all—and, with a great upward lift, threw him into a dive.

For lunch, the boys ate pieces of sliced cantaloupe, tuna sandwiches, and barbequed potato chips from small bags. They drank apple juice from small boxes. The radio was playing what Scott called "summer songs"; and those certain songs always reminded him of summer. And every year, new songs were added.

Just then, a horsefly landed on Avery's arm. He looked at it and screamed in horror, "Greenhead!" Avery jumped up, throwing his juice box. His father looked over at him and smiled. He motioned for Avery to calm down. Avery ran around the chairs in circle, waving his arms over his head.

Horseflies were the greatest enemy of the summertime and, once spotted, became the greatest concern.

"If it bites you, it's poisonous. Ezra says they can suck out all your blood," Scott explained. "You can get gangrene, and they might even have to amputate your brain." Avery screamed, flailing everywhere, looking at his arms. Scott laughed at his brother, secretly watching his own arms to make sure none landed on him.

Just then, a woman with red hair walked up and talked with Scott's father. She was smiling and friendly and reminded Scott of his mother, only in a much different way. She spoke very nicely in a light, musical voice. Scott forgot about the horseflies and his brother and watched the woman with red hair and the white-and-yellow flowers of her baby blue bathing suit, as she turned and said, "Hello Avery. Hello Scott." Scott blushed and waved, "Hi."

His father suggested that the ocean really is the only great defense against the greenheads. Scott looked toward Avery then the ocean. He saw the skittering form of a fly and that odd half-jump half-flight that the large greenheads do. He then jumped up and ran toward the water.

On his way down, he studied a lifeguard in orange shorts and white hat with blue zinc on the nose blow a whistle at kids playing with body boards in the water. The whistle then fell, and the lifeguard twirled it on his fingers and returned to the tall chair behind him, trailing the shiny red life preserver labeled GUARD.

Scott imagined climbing the tall orange chair and looking and seeing all the kids playing on the beach. He dreamed of blowing the whistle and telling everyone to get out of the water—*SHARK!*—and of the orange life preserver and how long he could float with it.

Avery, calm now, played in the shallows with a gray shovel and yellow bucket, filling the bucket with sand and pouring it back into the water. Scott did not feel like playing with Avery, so he went on his own to practice holding his breath. He wanted to increase his endurance for his career with Cousteau.

The tide emerged, exposing corrugated sands as low tide got nearer, and the water receded. Scott swam out and floated in the gentle current. Noticing this, he held his breath for forty-five seconds, and upon reaching ninety, he would return and announce the news. Scott kicked under the waves, popping his masked face up through the foam to replenish his breath and then slipped back down. He reached seventy-three seconds and popped his head up. He had drifted for some time, and the swift current carried him closer to the rocky part of the beach. He saw he was now by a different lifeguard chair, near rocks and shallows of the Tides Restaurant. He spotted his father's unique walk and saw the woman with the red hair and baby blue bathing suit walking toward the slush stand at the end of the beach. Scott began the inhales and exhales necessary to try for ninety seconds again. As he did, he watched the woman and his father stop near the stand, embrace, and then kiss.

Scott held his inhalation and watched. He did not submerge. He thought of what Ezra said about crabs kissing. He remembered his mother and kissing her at the airport a few days before. He began talking to himself about it, saying, you want to fly on an airplane when you go to the airport if that airplane takes your mother and goes to California and flies high over your house. You did not remember your father kissing your mother or saying anything. You only asked your father to show you where California was on your globe and did not ask what business she had but did ask why she flew without you. Scott inhaled again and submerged.

He held his breath. You must concentrate on holding your breath and not thinking. You should not think about anything, especially the pressure of the held breath. Just count slowly until you cannot and your lungs rebel, and it forces you to breathe. But do not. Do not breathe. Hold it, and do not. You cannot breathe water even if it is lovely and cold. Maybe you could if you were a fish. If only you were a fish. Let the air out slowly as bubbles, like that of a fish, and the aching will go away. Then you are empty, and your lungs ache; and you can only thrust upward, breathe, and fill yourself with air.

Scott held his breath and counted to ninety-two before he stood. He moved to the shallower water. He was very proud of the ninety-two and knew that with practice, he would be working for Cousteau in no time.

There were many children playing in the shallows and throwing sand. Scott grew irritated at them and their game and their not understanding his need to rest after training. He wanted to swim back to empty waters. As he noted his direction, calculating his bearings, he spotted his father's walk. His dad was with the red and blue woman. Scott stopped and watched. He could not help but stare at the woman, embarrassed and at the same time fascinated with her red hair and baby blue bottom, as he remembered napping his head on his mother's bottom, recalling how soft and comfortable it was and how silly and comical people's bottoms were. Scott did not want his father to see him, so he turned and swam in the direction of the rocks.

He surfaced and walked ashore, passing the lifeguards on the hot dry sand and then up the hot asphalt pathway to the Tides. The Tides Restaurant sold ice cream and french fries. Scott liked to eat them at the same time. It was something about the salt and the sweet.

While thinking, he watched a female lifeguard in orange with a whistle seated on her high orange chair. He wanted to return to his shoes and get some money for a bouncing ball, but he was thinking all the time about the "red-and-blue" woman and his father.

Scott walked to the shallows, and as he stepped, a young girl shouting startled him.

"Don't step there!" a girl's voice screamed.

"What?" Scott recoiled, startled.

"You almost stepped on it! See!" A girl with straight brown hair and big smile of crooked front teeth pointed to a crab scuttling sideways along the bottom. She leant down, thrusting her tanned arm underwater, but the crab moved quickly out of her reach.

"Missed!" she yelled then tried again, but the crab dug in and showed its large claw in the sand, and it vanished.

"Grab it from behind," Scott said.

"I can't see it!" Her crooked teeth puckered.

"Use this!" Scott handed the girl his diving mask. As he did, she smiled, and Scott saw her eyes. They were bright and blue and full of fun things. They were full of sapphire. They sparkled in the sun. Scott saw stars falling all around her head—silver, gold, and blue. Who was she? Scott watched her snap the strap of the diving mask over her hair and adjust it on her nose. She smiled at him then thrust her head, facedown, into the water. The crab's slick chitin legs flayed open, but she grabbed it. She withdrew it from the water. The large claws reached outward as she held it immobile. Scott smiled. It was orange and white underneath, and it had funny eyes. The girl pulled off Scott's diving mask, dropped it in the water, and walked away. She didn't say anything. Scott picked up his mask and followed her to the shallows where she had a green bucket filled with seawater. She lowered her prize into the bucket then introduced herself to Scott.

"I'm Audrey. Audrey Wilde."

Scott sat next to her and looked in the bucket.

"My name's Scott."

"Scott! Look at his claw! Scott!" Audrey pointed at the crab and smiled. "Scott! Doesn't she look happy in her new home?"

Scott looked. The crab did not look too particularly happy.

"How old are you?" Audrey asked.

"Seven," Scott answered.

"I'm five and three quarters," Audrey said.

"See if it will grab the snorkel," Scott said, handing it to Audrey. She obliged and thrust the snorkel at the crab. It ignored the snorkel and tried to run but was trapped within the bucket. Then Audrey screamed, "We should find her a boy, Scott! And see if they kiss!"

"Why would they kiss?" He pretended to know nothing of the subject. He looked at her funny. How did she know?

"Everyone knows if you hold two crabs close, they kiss, duh!" Audrey laughed.

"There are more crabs by the rocks over there." Scott pointed. Audrey jumped up and began running toward the rocks.

"I'm not supposed to go there!" Scott yelled. He felt very immature saying those words considering Audrey was younger than him. He thought of his father and his warning, but then thoughts of Cousteau and his training came to him. He stood silent. For some reason, it was hard for him to think. He watched Audrey. There was something strange about her. It was as if Audrey were filled with a song that he could not stop listening to. He could not figure it out. It was the music that intoxicates and destroys adults or marries them for life. Few men can survive a collision with a woman forged in the heart of a star. For a moment, Scott saw into the future, to his adult world as a man; and there in its sky, Audrey's eyes hovered, brilliant and shining, like two bright stars on the deck of an ether ship in the sky. Her voice called for him to follow, like the sound of the ocean that calls to sailing men. He felt as if he should lash himself with strong ropes to a lifeguard chair and wrap his ears with a beach towel, lest the sound drive him mad with pleasure. Scott felt afraid, but there was no need to fear. The voice did not come from a Siren, instead Audrey's voice burst out of the foundations of the deep sea, rising and rolling to sun and sky. If Atlas carried the world, Audrey's voice was the sound he marched to. Such it was to Scott, yet he could not explain it, though it conquered him completely.

"I'm coming! Wait!" Scott ran after her.

Scott and Audrey ran toward the shaggy, seaweed-covered rocks. She asked him to carry her green bucket, and he agreed. For that, she held his hand. Scott was delighted. Large houses sat baking in the sun, and Scott and Audrey walked by as she read a posted wooden sign Keep Out! Private Beach. Audrey screamed, jumped at Scott, and laughed, "That means you, Scott!"

The clear expired levels of the waves rolled past their feet. The last of the water turned to small bubbles rolling gritty bits of blue mussels and broken barnacles, and Scott put the bucket down and followed Audrey, wading out to the rocks and deeper water.

The sand under Scott's feet mashed like gritty dough and felt cold between his toes. His feet sank into the soft sand up to his ankle, and he imagined sinking into it up to his waist and wished he had a rope and would make a lasso and use it if that happened. The water was warmer here; and the large rocks, gray in the sun like great stone beast's backs, were draped with whiskered weeds and slippery with brine. All around there were dull brownish green rockweeds drying in the sun or floating in the waters.

Scott was careful to avoid the barnacles on the rocks and moved his feet away from the puffs of algae and red seaweeds on the bottom, and dragged his legs until he was waist deep in the water then put his mask on and submerged. The larger rocks were jagged with sharp edges and sea grass, and under them, Scott found urchins and snails. Audrey moved a flap of brown seaweed and, in the turbid water near a large stone, found two starfish. She held them up, showing them to Scott.

"Scott! Look! They are stars! One for each of us! See? This one is for you! This one's for me!"

Scott smiled and thanked her. He continued searching for crabs in places that Audrey would not put her fingers, and he moved large pieces of brown fucus and thrust his hand into the small crevasses.

"There's one, Scott!" Audrey screamed. Scott thrust his hand under, grabbing at the crab. The crab was very angry and pursed its antennae, offering up a large claw.

"Watch out!" Audrey warned, her crooked teeth lively.

"Look at this one!" Scott had managed to grab it from behind and pull it out of the water.

"You got one, Scott! One with whiskers!" She laughed.

"He's upset," Scott said.

"Scott, let's see, he'll kiss Nina!" Audrey ran, reached in her green bucket, and carefully removed the orange crab.

"Who's Nina?" Scott asked, holding his whiskered crab carefully.

"Scott! Nina's my other crab! She's named after La Niña! My mom says that's a storm that's a crabby storm that makes rain." Audrey ran back and held Nina up front of the whiskered crab. The two crabs sat motionless.

"Try it closer," Scott urged. Audrey moved the orange crab closer. For a moment, Scott thought the crabs would kiss, but the whiskered crab thrust and snapped at Audrey's thumb. She dropped the orange crab, jerking her hand, screaming.

"Sorry!" Scott said to her. "You all right?"

"Scott! He's getting away!" Audrey shouted, pointing at the orange crab scuttling along the bottom.

"I'll get him." Scott dropped the whiskered crab and went after the orange one. He put his mask on, reached down into the water, and grabbed it. The old whiskered crab ran away. Scott stood up.

"Scott! You got her! Nina!" Audrey held the bucket up, and Scott dropped the crab in. While doing that, he felt something walk over his toes. He looked down in the water with his mask and spotted a small brown shell with white legs moving along the bottom.

He lifted the hermit crab by the spiral valves of its shell. The inside was polished pink and smooth as pearl; and the hermit crab withdrew, leaving only the tips of its claws, stalk eyes, and two antennas visible. Scott held it and examined it, feeling the crab's stridulations.

Scott sat with her in the shallows by the bucket. He listened to her sing. An adult woman with tanned strong arms walked over to them. She looked very much like Audrey and was smiling. Scott heard her say some things to Audrey, then,

"And who is this nice young man?"

"That's Scott."

Audrey's mother turned to Scott smiling,

"Hello Scott. Aren't you a handsome young man."

Scott blushed and said nothing. He felt very shy.

"Audrey, I want you out of the water for a little bit so we can put more sunscreen on you. I don't want you to burn."

"OK mommy."

"Nice to meet you Scott."

"Bye." Scott said and hearing the word sunscreen, he remembered his father. He had to get back. He watched Audrey's mother hand Audrey a toy boat and a green pirate's bandana before returning to a group of other women who were standing and talking. Scott watched Audrey play with a small white toy sailboat. He put the hermit crab in his pocket and moved closer to her.

Audrey sat in the shallow water, pushing the sailboat in her hands. She wore the green pirate's bandana and was leaning, blowing her breath into the boat's plastic sails. She told Scott that he must call her captain and that the starfish would ride together in the sailboat. Scott watched Audrey place the two starfish in the small plastic boat and push it around until a large wave capsized it and both starfish slid overboard. Scott picked up the starfish and handed them to Audrey. She looked at him and said, "Scott, you know what? I'm going to marry you, you know."

"What? Marry me? No. I have to go back now," Scott said very seriously. He looked at her. She was smiling, and she took her captain's hat off and threw it, singing to starfish in her hand.

"Not now, Scott!" Audrey stopped singing, looked at him, and laughed. Scott blushed. He stood, taking out the hermit crab. He could not figure anything to say, so he showed it to her. Audrey started sang again, and her voice in the air like wind in a storm that fills the sky, leaving the earth very changed. He listened to Audrey as he turned to walk away. She waved to him, smiling.

"Scott darling. Scott! Don't forget your star." Audrey stood with her hand extended, her voice all music and charm.

"I have to get going, my dad's going to kill me."

"Scott, take it! Take your star!" Audrey leaned forward, and as she handed him the starfish, she kissed his cheek. The group of older women with Audrey's mother saw this and let out a round of "awes!" and "that's so cute!"

Scott felt the hot deep red blush fill his cheeks. He looked at Audrey, embarrassed and shy, blushing, with a dizzy spin in his head. She smiled. He could not speak, so he turned and ran away.

"Bye, Scott! Scott! Bye!" Audrey's voice followed him down the beach, then vanished.

Scott held the hermit crab and the starfish and ran fast through the shallows back to where the sand was harder. He ran along past many people playing in the shallows. Children bodysurfed in the breaking waves, and others ran stomping and jumping in the foam. A few were sitting in the shallows, digging and using buckets. Scott stopped for a moment to fix the mask and snorkel that sat around his neck then ran down the beach toward his father's chair.

He spotted his father walking that funny walk by the water's edge and saw Avery beside him. They were standing, throwing the purple football back and forth.

"Scott? Where have you been? We were looking for you," Scott's father said.

Scott did not answer.

"Look." Scott presented his father with the starfish and the hermit crab. "I met Audrey and found crabs and am getting married and I held my breath for ninety-two seconds!"

"I told Avery a shark ate you. I told the lifeguard if he found you to throw you back."

Scott looked at his father and told him the time he held his breath again. The starfish and the hermit crab were sitting in his outstretched hand. Avery saw them and screamed, "I want a sta'fish and 'ermit crab!"

Scott hid them.

His father spoke, "You held your breath for a minute and a half. You've been gone an hour." He looked at Avery.

"No. We have to go now. Throw them back, Scott. Come on!"

"I want a sta'fish!" Avery pulled at his father's shorts, twisting and hanging.

"Scott, we're going to go. Grab the football. Throw them back, and let's go." Scott's father walked back to his chair. Scott looked at the starfish then at the hermit crab. He took a deep breath, hid the starfish in his pocket then raised his arm, cocked his shoulder like his favorite baseball player, and threw the hermit crab far and high toward the waves.

"Scott!" his father called.

Hearing his father, Scott turned and followed. He thought about his victory in holding his breath, the two starfish riding in the sailboat and the crabs not kissing, and then of Audrey Wilde. She was his first kiss. He felt taller and much older. He touched the starfish in his pocket.

The hermit crab, falling high and fast through the air, plopped down into the waves. A gull with its hard yellow eyes and lean white-and-gray body circled with its black wing tips spinning, then dove, following the brown-and-pink shell into the crashing of the foam.

SUMMERTIME

The summer goes too quickly after spring,
All of us budding in the heat. Autumn
Will be here soon enough so let us swim,
Brown bodies on the beach into the waves.

When I first noticed her upon the sand,
Years passed before she noticed me;
But as a seagull spying from the land,
I followed near the waves' thundering feet.

She reminded me of one my arms adored,
Darling, may I, darling, just one kiss?
Two starfish sailing 'round a shallow ford.
Is it mermaids that are singing or is it that kiss?

The winter comes too quickly each to each,
As summer wanes with nimbus from our reach.

WHEN WE WERE GODS

"Scotty, where do you hear those stories?" Scott's father laughed. Scott was telling him about the Woodlawn Cemetery and the rumors of rabbits living there that could speak. "You just read *Watership Down*, that's where you got this. There's nothing in Woodlawn but mourners and gardeners." The FM radio blasted Van Halen's, *Beautiful Girls*, as they drove. "When you get to Ezra's, be careful around the pool. I don't want you running around and cracking your head open. And don't forget to thank Mrs. Mann for letting you stay."

"I will," Scott said.

"Tomorrow, I'll pick you up at around three o'clock."

"OK."

"Do you have your inhaler?"

"Yes."

"Be sure to remember to keep it with you and not to lose it."

"I know."

"You know the house number to reach me." Scott rolled his eyes.

Scott's father pulled the car over in front of Ezra's house. It was a black Mercedes with tinted windows. He put his hand on Scott's head as Scott unfastened his seat belt and gathered his things.

"All right, Scott. Have fun."

Scott watched Ezra run down the driveway toward the car. He got very excited seeing Ezra and grabbed his backpack, opened the car door, and jumped out.

"Scott! Here's some money."

Scott climbed back into the car. His father handed him a twenty-dollar bill.

"OK. Put that away."

"Thanks."

"Give us a kiss." Scott hid the twenty dollars in his pocket, then leaned over the seat and gave his father a kiss on the cheek. Scott then jumped out of the car and said good-bye, slinging his bag over his shoulder. Ezra appeared beside him. He was smiling. He waved to Scott's dad and then laughed.

"Give us a kiss!" Ezra said, trilling his voice.

"Shut up!"

"Took you long enough! The pool's evaporated already."

"I couldn't come right away. Avery needed a ride to Little League."

"Come on!"

Scott followed Ezra up the driveway. Ezra's house was at the top of Reservoir Avenue, the tallest hill in Revere. The hill overlooked Revere all the way to Saugus on one side and Chelsea, East Boston, and Boston Harbor on the other. The house was a white two story at the top of a steep driveway. Behind the house was a built-in pool. The front door was never opened, so Scott always entered either through the back by the pool or from the side through the garage. Today they entered through the garage.

The door from the garage opened into a sort of pathless room where Ezra's father, a retired air force pilot, set up his hunting trophies, helmets, and assortments of oddities such as animal skins, meat-curing jars, and helicopter photographs. The room was called a playroom by Ezra and had some of Ezra's toys in it but was really not a playroom at all—always smelled funny and, in the heat, smelled more because Ezra's family only air-conditioned the upstairs. The room smelled mostly of Schnauzer.

Schnauzer literally was a giant schnauzer, an enormous beast of a dog, with a black coat like coal and large paws and human-sized head. The house was Schnauzer's, especially the playroom, and he would bark and get all into everything. Scott feared Schnauzer for the dog would bark, play, and lick; and the licks would make Scott wheeze. He was allergic to animals, and it got worse when he was excited.

From outside Ezra's house, it looked simple as any other house along Reservoir Avenue, but inside the walls were constructed of exposed logs. The kitchen was a laboratory of jarred spices and meats that Scott assumed Ezra's father had hunted and killed. On the wall between the kitchen and the playroom, there were boiled shark jaws, a deer's head with antlers, a moose's head with even larger antlers, and a bear's head with no antlers at all. There were photographs of helicopters, of Ezra's father in the military, and of strange men in mirrored sunglasses with guns—fishing and holding fish.

Through the kitchen was the living room that was a complete mystery to Scott. It resembled photographs Scott had seen of his great-great-grandmother's house. There was an enormous chandelier over a glass coffee table. The rug was thick and white mink fur, and the sofa was cream-colored leather. A giant fireplace occupied the entire wall opposite the entrance. Scott was convinced a secret door sat behind it. The wall of the living room was decorated with hanging portraits of Ezra's family in oil paint, and the eyes of the portrait of Ezra's grandmother followed whoever entered the living room.

Set on the fireplace mantle were gold-sculptured lions with eyes of shiny jewels and many other small oddities that resembled pirate's treasure to Scott. A large grandfather clock ticked its pendulum swings, and a large jade cat stood on the rug like a sentry amidst polished trees.

There was one treasure that far surpassed all the jewels, statues, or paintings of Ezra's house; and that was Ezra's eighteen-year-old sister, Elizabeth. Ezra's sister had long, curly, mermaid-blond hair and hazel eyes. She was running around in capris and a shoulder-string tank top with a towel on her head, laughing and talking to the phone that she balanced between her ear and shoulder. Scott watched her walk in and out of strings of green glass beads strung along an arch separating the door to her room. The beads made a characteristic clicking whenever passed through, and Scott's ears always listened for it. Elizabeth was supposedly a witch, according to Ezra, and Scott believed it.

Scott never told Ezra about his feelings for Elizabeth. Only once did he show interest in her by suggesting that they set an adventure in her room; but Ezra was not interested, she being his older sister who made fun of him. Scott, therefore, never set foot in Elizabeth's room; and to him, it was Aphrodite's pedestal on Mount Olympus.

Years later, when in high school and rumors of Ezra's sister sunbathing nude spread through the freshman boy's gossip, Scott never made joke but remembered Elizabeth's room and the wonder of it. And the rumor, if true, was only a concurrence to the allure that she forever had.

Scott and Ezra were not allowed into the living room as everything in there was covered with plastic, even the rug, but they had to walk through it to get to the stairs that led up to Ezra's room.

Upstairs, Ezra's room was large and spacious with a bunk bed in the corner and posters of WWII airplanes and bikini models on the walls. Ezra built model cars and displayed them on his bureau. He painted the cars expertly to resemble the real things. There were a black 1959 Chevy Impala, a yellow 1921 Ford Model T racer, a blue 1968 Ford Mustang, a red 1932 Ford Deuce Coupe, and a white 1962 Corvette convertible. Team flags of the New England Patriots and a poster of Bo Derek from the movie *10* resided on the back of Ezra's door.

Scott examined Bo Derek every time he entered. He did not enjoy her as much as Batgirl on the television show, *Batman*. He made fun of how much Ezra liked Deborah Harry, the singer.

The pride and joy of Ezra's room was Ezra's rifle. It was a replica Brown Bess musket with a forty-six-inch Long Land barrel, the kind carried and used by Paul Revere and the early American colonists when they began their war against England for independence. Its barrel was set on a walnut stock and underneath the ramrod. You could pull the rotating cock back and press the trigger, and the cock would strike the L-shaped frizzen with a snap. And always, Scott would ask Ezra to take it down off the wall so he could hold it and sight it and pretend he was being rushed by the Red Coats. However, he did not today.

Ezra assumed his position under the gun as he knew it was coming, but nothing came; so Ezra took the gun down anyway and began to sight it, making noises of approaching battle. Scott opened his backpack. Today he carried a surprise: a replica .45-caliber handgun he had loaned from his friend James. In Scott's backpack, he usually carried a series of adventuring essentials. Everything he might need—a pocket watch, a handkerchief, a flashlight, a silver compass, a swiss army knife (he had lost the toothpick and tweezers), an astronaut's pen (that could write upside down), a small pad of paper (for drawing maps), a cigarette lighter, a marble bag filled with sand, and an inhaler (Scott was asthmatic). But today, he also had James' gun.

"You be the Red Coats," Scott said, pulling the gun out. "I will be the American army in World War II." He held up James's gun. Ezra put his rifle down.

"Where did you get that?"

"I borrowed it from James."

"You're not going to shoot me, are you?"

"No! It doesn't fire."

"It's real?"

"It was. See how you can remove the magazine and cock the hammer and even slide this back." Scott manipulated the gun, and as he did, he was very proud.

"Does it shoot?"

"It doesn't fire. The barrel here is filled with metal."

"Let me try."

"All right." Scott handed the gun to Ezra. Ezra removed the magazine, slammed it back in, pulled back on back on the slide, sighted the gun, and pulled the trigger. The hammer slammed forward with a snap.

"Did James give this to you?" Ezra sounded jealous, and Scott played it up.

"Sort of. He gave it to me before he went to Florida with his family. I have it for the entire week he's in Disney World. It's the same gun his grandfather was killed with."

"He was killed by it?"

"No, he had it when he was shot. They filled it with lead after the war."

"Can I play with it?"

"Yeah, but do not tell Tom or Joe when they come over. Especially Joe. He would take it or try too."

"All right."

Schnauzer was out back by the pool when the boys ran down. Scott was a good swimmer and diver, but Ezra could do flips off the diving board and said he would teach Scott. Scott would learn for the day only to forget the next time.

Ezra never complained about teaching but would make fun of Scott's lanky attempts; and the two would laugh, and always, the lessons ended in a round of cannonballs. Ezra was very large for his age and could make a tremendous splash, and Scott always tried to beat him.

The boys swam, and Schnauzer ran, barking around the edge. Schnauzer would snap and bark at the water. Scott and Ezra targeted their splashes close to soak his black fur, and Schnauzer would escape across the grass, shaking his head and then his rump.

Ezra's mother barbequed, and they ate hamburgers and chinese sausages with red sweet-and-sour sauce, beef hot dogs, relish and ketchup. Scott talked about adventuring and had an idea for an expedition into the graveyard behind their friend Tom's house. It was the Woodlawn Cemetery, a strange place with strange lights along the river at night. There were whispered rumors of large colonies of rabbits enslaved by evil fallen hares. Hidden in the heart of the woods there, living under the tombs and graves, a community of hares ruled in secret. They could talk and understand English. The Fallen Ones they were called and they were larger than normal rabbits. They had red burning eyes and hunted and ate cats. The gentle and free rabbits, displaced due to construction and the growth of the graveyard, were easy prey for the Fallen Ones. Such a rumor apparently explained the lack of wildlife at the Woodlawn and Glenwood cemeteries.

It was about 2:00 PM when Tom and Joe arrived at Ezra's house. Tom and Joe were next-door neighbors and lived on Amelia Place. Ezra called Tom and explained Scott's plan for the adventure in the graveyard. He agreed but, because it was hot that day, decided to ride with Joe up to Ezra's and go swimming first. Tom and Joe were in Scott's class. Ezra was the same age but in a different class, and they have known each other since kindergarten. After Ezra, James was Scott's best friend; and after James, Tom. And today Tom had a surprise. Tom smiled.

"Tom, show Scotty your wrist rocket," Joe said. Tom obliged after checking the yard for Ezra's mother and pulled out a small device that looked like a slingshot.

"It's a slingshot?" Scott asked.

"No. It's a wrist rocket." Tom pointed to the perpendicular brace that was attached to the bottom. Scott scanned the black aluminum frame, the yellow elastic tubes, and the split leather pouch.

"How far does it shoot?" Ezra asked. He was looking too. Tom fitted a glass marble into the pouch, gripped the trigger bracing the frame on his wrist, pulled back, and sighted it at a tree.

"About a hundred yards."

"That far?" Scott looked at Ezra. Tom fired, and the yellow elastic whipped, and the marble shot thru the air. He handed the wrist rocket to Scott.

"Where did you get it?" Scott asked.

"My cousin who lives down South. He sent it to me. He's the one going into the Marines." Tom smiled.

"I'm going to join the air force and fly helicopters like my father," Ezra said.

"How'd he send it to you?" Scott asked.

"In the mail." Tom crunched a potato chip.

"Did it cost a lot?"

"Dunno."

"It shoots marbles far?"

"Yeah." Scott studied the wrist rocket. He imagined shooting bottles and wondered if it could take down a fighter plane. He told them, and they laughed. James's World War II gun lost its appeal to the wrist rocket's action. Ezra would not allow them to try shooting one of his models.

"My mother is coming. Put it away!" Ezra whispered. Scott handed the wrist rocket back to Tom. Tom folded it and hid it away. Scott talked of going to the graveyard and having an adventure there. The boys all agreed, but first, Joe and Tom wanted to jump in the pool.

Diving, jumping, pushing each other off the board, they played as the hot sun beat down. Ezra was the biggest and built like a bear. Scott was thin and tall and would help push Ezra in but always was pulled in himself. Joe had studied karate since he was four, was able to balance and alone could toss them all, even Ezra's bearlike body. Tom was heavy in the stomach and had good strength. He grabbed Joe by the legs, Ezra wrapped him under the arms, and Scott tipped them all over the edge.

Scott did not trust Joe because one time, while walking to Tom's house with Joe, Scott watched Joe steal a jacket from an open car. Scott warned him not to, but Joe reasoned that it was all right; and if the person really wanted to keep it, they would not have left it in an open car. Scott was careful around him ever since.

After swimming, the boys wrapped themselves in towels and sat, drying in the sun. Of all Scott's friends, Ezra was the best storyteller. Scott loved listening to Ezra's stories, but they were always better when Ezra spoke to a group. Tom was not as funny with a group as when alone and always got Scott laughing. Joe was the hardest to amuse, and if you made him laugh, he would treat you like his best friend until you made him upset and then you were no longer his friend. Ezra told the story about the ski trip where some boys had seen Alexandria Morley's leg break. Tom told the one about the food fight in the cafeteria between Marcus Dunn and Pauly Lette and how Eric Wasberg had laughed milk through his nose. They spoke of baseball and of bikes. They spoke of girls and who was easy to kiss.

Danielle was most kissable. But she kissed everyone. She would not kiss you though. Marlene was very kissable. She'd been kissing Dave. No. Yes. She'd been kissing Dave and got caught by Mr. Lipton. Tammy wants to kiss Scotty. Scotty does not want to kiss Tammy. He would rather kiss his hand. He would rather kiss his hand, and you would rather kiss your own feet. I would kiss Beth Anne's feet. You would kiss her feet after she had walked through mud. Scotty wants to kiss Audrey. Who is Audrey? Audrey Wilde, that girl Scott talks about. I don't know. Scott loves a ghost. I thought he loved Nicole Christopher. Nicole? No, well he likes her, but she kisses Jim Hicks. Besides, Scotty is too shy to kiss Nicole! We are all shy around Noel Valence. You are shy around fat Patricia Petulak. No! Yes! No! Yes! Yes! You are and have kissed her fat cheeks!

They all laughed. Tom had a fantastic laugh and always laughed at his own stories, and that got Ezra started. And once he started, he did not stop. Ezra was the easiest to make laugh, and he enjoyed laughing. And years later, after Ezra was killed fighting in the Middle East, Scott missed Ezra's laugh more than anything.

As soon as they were all dry, they grabbed their bikes and got ready to leave. To ride to Tom's house, they would follow Ezra's hill down to the Town Line Brook Canal behind Amelia Place that runs along the Middlesex and Suffolk County split. The canal is saltwater coming from the ocean at Revere Beach, becoming the Saugus River, then down becoming the Pines River, then winding through becoming the marshy lands by Route 60, following parallel to Washington Street where it continues with the Holy Cross Cemetery to the north, and the Glenwood and Woodlawn cemeteries to the south. The canal terminated around Lynn Street before it reached Route 99. The marshy lands of Revere and Saugus were largely undeveloped, as were a few areas at that time, and were the best place for adventurers with the exception of the dunes behind the North Gate shopping plaza.

The boys said good-bye to Ezra's mother, who urged them to ride carefully and told Ezra to call her from Tom's house. Everyone said thank-you to her and good-bye to Schnauzer, and standing on their bike pedals, they rode down Reservoir Avenue to Irving Street. They raced over to Adams Street, through the Coolidge Street housing projects, then up onto Cushman Avenue. That became Sergeant Street, and they rode under the Northeast Expressway, onto Washington Avenue, and then down onto Amelia Place to Tom's house.

The late-afternoon sun was hot, but now cumulus clouds moved in and would soon cover and make it dusk. Joe led the way, followed by Tom and Scott and then Ezra. They stopped for traffic on Washington Avenue. Tom loaded his wrist rocket and shot it at a tree. The marble exploded in a shower of glass.

At Tom's house, the boys parked their bikes and, after saying hello to Tom's mom, set off toward the canal through Tom's backyard. The plan was to cut along the river and make way into the cemetery. The rabbits supposedly had an underground labyrinth in the center where they lived in a vast city. The boys traveled toward the center, along through a brier, past porcupine tusks and catch weed. They kept clear of the wet earth and marsh, staying close to the spurs of the tag thorns and cone peaks, the thorny brush, and hedgehog tips until they saw the first gray stone and rust of the cemetery and then more headstones and the expanse of it.

Scott held his compass and steered them southwest as Ezra read off the old names on the tombs, and the other boys followed. Joe screamed and made rabbit noises with his teeth, and everyone would start and then laugh, and Tom pretended to be a zombie walking with a limp. They rounded the edge of one area, disappointed, for it came close to houses. They turned and moved back.

Their route proved bad again because of mourners, so they doubled back and decided on a different path that wound up a dark hill. Glenwood and Woodlawn cemeteries were large and contained many hills and dense trees. A number of the tombs in some areas were closely packed and dull gray. Some were decorated with flowers, and a few with photographs or other keepsakes. Other tombs were grown over with shrubs and shadows. The boys made their way into a deeper section marked by angel statues and a large willow tree. As they entered, a brown rabbit poked his head out and darted in front of them. It startled them all.

"A rabbit! Get it!" Joe yelled.

"No! Don't! We are here to help them. Don't hurt it! We want to follow it," Scott said.

"After it!" Joe yelled.

"They understand English, remember?" Scott whispered.

"Talking bunny! Where's your friends!" Tom laughed.

Tom fitted his wrist rocket with a marble, took aim, and fired. The marble smacked off the ground and shattered on a tomb. The boys chased after the rabbit with Tom repeating his fire. Marbles bounced off the grass and ricocheted into the headstones. The rabbit jumped, twitching its nose and its legs like springs, darted left and right.

The boys followed into a large dark brush then out into a copse occupied by rows of crumbling flat tombs. The rabbit kicked its spring legs and leapt, landing on the pads of its forelegs, and, using them as a pivot, kicked again. Marbles smacked off the tombs, snapping and cracking.

"Don't shoot at it!" Scott yelled at Tom. "We're here to help. That's obviously not a Fallen One. Leave it alone!" But Joe was encouraging Tom and the chase. He pointed to Tom and motioned for him to circle around and flank the rabbit.

"They'll never trust us if you hurt one," Scott implored. Joe said nothing. The rabbit halted under a tree, sniffing, hiding in the tree's roots. Its brown fur camouflaged it, but Tom spotted it and gave the signal to stop, and the boys held and got low to the ground.

"It's in that tree's roots."

"Leave it, Tom!" Scott yelled.

"You can move over there and take the shot." Joe pointed.

"Don't get wheezy, Scott," Joe mocked Scott.

"Screw you, Joe."

"It was your idea to come here." Joe put up his hands.

"So? To stop the Fallen Ones, not hurt this rabbit."

"Maybe it's a Fallen One. I'm going to look." Tom began to creep forward.

"Fallen Ones have red eyes, they're bigger." Then an idea occurred to Scott. He shouted to Tom, "Wait!" He grabbed Tom's shoulder. Tom squeezed his eyes to absorb the sound and then looked at Scott. The rabbit had not moved.

"What?" he said.

"Do it with this." Scott fumbled in his backpack and pulled out the World War II .45. Its nickel finish shined amidst the gray of the tombs. Tom's eyes widened, and Joe sat silent. Ezra smiled but quickly hid it. Scott pointed the gun at Tom, lowered it. Tom put his hands up.

"Good lord, Scott, don't shoot. Don't shoot!"

"Scott! What are you, psycho? Where'd you get *that*?" Joe could hardly speak.

"I took it from James' father's safe. Now you're going to listen to me, and do what I say, Tom." Scott looked at Ezra. Ezra went along.

"This gun was James' father's in the army. It's a United States Armed Forces automatic pistol." Scott had memorized the inscription on its side. "Model of 1911A1 caliber .45."

Tom swallowed and closed his eyes.

"Jesus, Scotty, don't you know kids aren't supposed to play with guns?" Joe said in a hushed voice.

Scott looked at Tom to see if he was understood. Tom opened his eyes, looked at the gun, then closed them again. Scott spoke, "OK, Tom, pay attention." He raised the gun. Tom lowered his hands and opened his eyes. Scott removed the magazine and slammed it back in then pulled on the slide and cocked the hammer. The gun was very large and very heavy, and the sound of it was convincing.

"James's grandfather killed Japanese with it in World War II." And as if that was the missing piece, the boys accepted it and looked to Scott for the next move. He spoke.

"If it really is a Fallen One, you'll need this." Scotty offered Tom the gun. Tom held still. He looked at it then took the gun and handed Scott his wrist rocket.

"Don't aim the gun this way!" Scott yelled, stuffing the wrist rocket into his backpack. Tom held the gun weakly in front of him and crawled forward. The rabbit sat still in the roots of the large tree.

Scott smiled and spoke to himself, "Do not worry, Mr. Rabbit. That gun cannot hurt you. You are a good one, aren't you? You are just like us, I bet—just scared and trying to live in peace." He watched Tom creep forward through the shrubs.

Scott watched, and just at that moment, Ezra whispered loudly, "Police! Police car!" All the boys ducked down. Tom ducked and rolled over toward the rabbit. Joe stood, looking, and Ezra fell down and hid. Kids were not allowed to play in the cemetery. It was considered trespassing, and the police enforced it.

Scott held his breath, then heard Tom move and a smack of a glass marble, and looked. There were no police. He looked over toward the rabbit. It was gone.

Tom stood with the .45 in his hand. Joe ran to where Tom stood, near the rabbit's tree, a bank of ferns. Ezra walked over and stood, examining something on the ground. Scott ran up next to Ezra and saw it was the rabbit.

"How? How did you?" He looked and saw Joe holding a similar rocket in his hand. He understood.

Tom looked at Scott then at Joe. Joe spoke, "I didn't tell you I brought one too. I found it at a flea market."

Scott did not say anything.

"You look like you're going to cry, Scott."

Ezra walked over. "Leave Scott alone, Joe."

Joe looked at Ezra, then scowled.

"Fine."

Scott kneeled by the rabbit. The marble struck behind its ear. Scott looked at the soft brown fur, the ears, and the underside that was as white as the legs lay long, stretched out and limp. He saw one of that rabbit's feet was larger than the other. Scott found a marble lying in the grass. He grabbed it and threw it at Tom.

"You killed it. It's dead."

"Is it dead?"

"Yeah. It's dead."

"Wow." Tom looked at Joe.

"You killed it alright," Scott said, looking.

"Don't get all asthmatic on us, Scott. This was your idea."

"This wasn't my idea. I came here to help, not kill them." Scott glared at Joe. Ezra looked around nervously.

"I saw another police car drive by," Ezra whispered.

"Cops will arrest us if they find us." Joe laughed.

"They'll arrest you for killing a rabbit." Scott returned. Joe laughed.

"I'll jus' tay I t'ought it was rabbit season." Joe joked in his best Looney Tunes—Elmer Fudd voice.

"Or is it duck season?" Joe continued, slapping Tom on the back of the head, beginning the old Looney Tunes joke. Tom played right along.

"Wabbit season!"

"Duck season!"

"Wabbit season!"

"Duck season!"

Scott ignored them, bent down, and picked up the rabbit.

"Where are you going, Scott?" Joe laughed.

"To bury it."

Joe raised his wrist rocket and placed a marble in the strap, aimed at a gravestone near Scott, and pulled the rubber bands as far back as he could. He loosed the marble, and it smacked, exploding white and powder.

"Forget you." Scott walked off.

"Don't take your wabbit and go!" Joe yelled.

This time, a police car drove by close and slowed. The remaining boys stopped and looked at each other and then ran. Tom threw the .45 into the river as he ran. Ezra followed him for a while then ran after Scott. Joe vanished into the undergrowth.

"This way." Ezra led Scott up behind a hill, over and around and then back out into a concealed copse. Scott spoke, "We've got to bury it, Ezra. What happened isn't right."

"We?"

"It wasn't right."

"How can you hold that rabbit? I thought you were allergic?"

"Dunno."

"What about the police?"

"If the police come, we'll run." Ezra and Scott ran into a sheltered copse. At the center was a large tree. Scott picked a spot near the tree to bury the rabbit. He laid the dead rabbit down on the ground, reached into his backpack, and took out his swiss army knife. He snapped out the spoon and began to dig. Ezra watched.

"We'll need a nice branch for this rabbit's headstone." Scott dug until he moved enough earth, then used his hands; and when the hole was deep enough, he snapped back the shovel.

"Give me that," Ezra said, looking at the knife.

"Why?"

"I watched my dad do this a hundred times. I'll cut you his lucky foot."

"What?"

"Hold this. Don't worry."

Scott watched Ezra.

Ezra pressed the blade onto the joint of the rabbit's largest foot and pulled. Scotty watched the cutting of sinews and the tendons. Blood wet the blade and seeped into the dirt. Ezra cut the last of the skin and, when finished, wiped the blade on the grass. He folded the knife and handed it back to Scott.

Ezra wrapped the rabbit's foot in Scott's handkerchief and handed it to him. Scott took Tom's wrist rocket and laid it next to the rabbit in the hole. Scott figured he should say something, so he spoke to himself. Rabbit, may you find peace. Please do not be angry. People can be stupid. However, not all of us are. Remember instead the sky, the land, and life that were yours: the time when we were gods, and brothers.

Scott pushed soil over and pressed it and marked it with the branch chosen by Ezra.

"Let's go," Scott said. The boys ran out of the cemetery down and away toward Fuller Street then Jefferson Drive, then down Cushman Avenue toward Broadway.

"Tom is going to be upset about his wrist rocket," Ezra said.

"Yeah."

"So is James. Do you have his gun?"

"No. Tom has it, I think."

"I saw him throw it into the river when he ran."

"Oh."

"You don't sound like you care." Ezra walked. Scott laughed then added, "I don't. It was dangerous even the way it was disabled. I'm glad it's gone."

"Where are our bikes?"

"Tom's house."

Scott felt the rabbit's foot in his pocket. He walked, looking at the sky to the dusk of orange and deep red.

"How long do I have to dry this?"

"Like a month," Ezra said. Scott was silent.

"A month, huh?" Scott said, feeling the rabbit's foot.

"My dad says those are real lucky."

Scott was silent. Suddenly, he realized he was thirsty and very hungry.

"I'm hungry," Ezra said as if reading his mind.

"Me too."

"We could go back to my house."

Scott looked in his pocket and pulled out the twenty-dollar bill.

"Let's go get some burgers. My treat."

The two walked down the street with a lightened step.

"Do you think anything happened to Tom and Joe?" Ezra asked.

"Nope."

A SONNET FOR THE LOST

Soldier, sir, where did you go? I see the
World despair. Fair eyes tearful and with woe
Where did you go, sir? Where? Beyond the stars
And moon? Remembrance flees from me. Where go?
I see the silent ships set for the West;
The sun stands high, yet colorless today;
It is springtime, but we seem in winter's crest,
No wind, no words, yet birdsong lightly play.
Did your footsteps find their friends of old,
Walking along shrouded ways? Your face unseen;
Your voice unheard; your heart, in ours, still bold;
In birth a boy, in life a man, in sleep
    For you our love unceasingly remains,
      But we'll miss you and your character of fame.

WITH ZANE AT THE TOWN LINE

I took my lucky rabbit's foot and headed out the front door. I was avoiding my father for I was not working but playing billiards for money, and he was angry. I wiped my eyes with my sleeve. I had been thinking about Ezra. I was trying to stop crying, but I could not. I felt guilty. Maybe he'd still be alive if I were with him. Maybe things could have been different. There's so many people in the world, it didn't seem fair. He died in the war in the Middle East, on the other side of the world.

It was raining steadily outside. I inhaled deeply. I needed some escape, some release, or I would go crazy with grief. It was cool out for summertime. I was nervous my dad would come home. I put on my good shoes and tied them tight. I looked at myself in the mirror, wiping my eyes. Great, I thought. I turned out the lights and walked down the stairs.

I picked the mail off the table and looked through for any with my name. There were none. I returned them to the table and went outside. The sky was thin and gray, with thick clouds that made the trees dark in their branches. The rain was cool and steady. I began walking. I headed down the street toward Broadway, the main street. I was meeting my friend, Tom.

I walked down the street with my hands in my pockets. Behind me, I heard footsteps in the rain. I stopped and turned around. There, in the cool light rain, walked an attractive woman. She was dressed all black—black shoes, a black hat, and a black lacy umbrella. She looked familiar. So familiar. Why? I could not place her. Thinking about it now, she looked like John Singer Sargent's Madame X. But back then, I did not know much art. She did not stop, but smiled at me. She was very beautiful—her hair dark, her skin alabaster; and as she walked by, it was as if my breath stopped. All at once, I felt very strange. My vision blurred, and I almost fell over. I felt faint and sick, as if I had been struck with a blow by a sword. I looked at her right into her eyes. She had black irises and black pupils that shone like two black stars in a black firmament. Or were they? They seemed to be pools of deep black water that held something from an ancient and earlier age of the world. I heard myself apologize for staggering. I struggled to stay standing. She nodded and continued, slowly walking away, water beading off her black umbrella and falling near her feet.

Then she was gone. The woman in black. Where was she? The dizziness passed. My senses returned. I pushed my hands back into my pockets and felt the rabbit's foot. Did that just happen or was it a dream? I could not tell. I began walking.

I passed by my neighbor's new car. It was a convertible Mercedes. I don't know the year, but it was older. It was beautiful and green. I hoped my lucky rabbit's foot would help me get one someday. I imagined the rabbit's foot was the wishing cap of Fortunatus. Something might be down there, deep down, I hoped. I felt only worn fur and dried skin. I walked, thinking of that.

Up Malden Street, I walked toward Broadway and the White Hen store. I was meeting Tom in the parking lot. I walked with my head down past the corner of Malden and Broadway and watched the cars pass, then crossed and turned right, walking by the Dairy Queen across Cushman Avenue to the White Hen.

Tom pulled in a few minutes later. He was driving his sister's car. It was a 1977 Chevrolet Camaro Sport Coupe, with a sparkly metallic baby blue paint job and white leather interior, Blaupunkt radio, and a dark stain on the front left hood from where Tom's sister hit and killed a Hoary bat. I tapped a square pack of menthol cigarettes against my palm then pulled the gold cellophane string, and the plastic cover fell away. Tom's sister did not smoke, and you could not smoke in her car. Tom opened his door and got out to join me for a smoke.

"'Sup, Scott!" He smiled with his wolf's nose. He reached for a cigarette, and I handed him the pack. He held a cigarette to his mouth and lifted a stainless steel lighter from his pocket.

"What's up?" I asked. He lit my cigarette with a flick of his hand. I could smell the lighter fluid as I took a long drag.

"You look like you saw a ghost."

I did not mention the woman in black.

"Just thinking about Ezra."

"I know. What a terrible accident. He was a good guy."

"Yeah. They're going to memorialize him at Arlington National Cemetery with other casualties from the Gulf War." Tom saw me, and my eyes screw up, and he changed the subject.

"How's your dad? He on you again?" He took a drag on his cigarette. I just smoked and nodded.

"Yeah, he said he's going to kick me out if I don't get a job." We watched the cars drive by on Broadway, their black wheels rolling hard on the wet street.

"What should we do?" Tom asked.

"Play some pool. Win some money. It's worse when I have to ask him for money."

"Where's your cue?"

"My father took it. He says billiards is a waste of time. He wants me to go to college, be a doctor. Says I'm too smart to waste my life."

"And God bless you then." Tom laughed.

I held my cigarette, trying not to waste my life, and Tom stood perfectly happy too. He was smiling. Under certain light, his nose looked more severe, and now it was enormous.

"I was just watching *Butch Cassidy and the Sundance Kid*," Tom said as he took a drag.

"I like that film," I said. I remembered the first time I watched it and the end where Paul Newman and Robert Redford run out against the entire Bolivian army, not knowing it is the entire army and thinking it is just a few police with pistols. I believed Butch and Sundance could take them. I knew they could not, but I wanted them to. The film did not show their deaths, only their last run, and you only hear them being shot. It was a kind of dignity, and I liked Paul Newman and Robert Redford more after, and Bolivians less.

"I see your sister let you use her car." I pointed to the Camaro.

"I got her some weed, and she loaned it to me."

"Nice."

The sun broke through a little during the ride to the Town Line, filtering through the high thin clouds. We drove up Cushman Avenue, crossing Newhall Street to Sergeant Street, turning right onto Washington Avenue and then onto Fuller Street. We drove past the monuments of the Glenwood and Woodlawn cemeteries on our left and the gray stones of the Holy Cross Cemetery to our right, and Malden was brown and gray, and we passed silent the resting plots of the two cemeteries.

We listened to Van Halen's 5150 on the cassette player. Sammy Hagar was the new singer and the song, *Dreams*, was blasting very loud. I turned the radio volume down.

"I like this album a lot, but the old Van Halen with David Lee Roth will always rule."

Tom nodded and turned the radio volume back up.

On Route 99, crossing Route 60, we continued until the rusted white Town Line Billiard and Bowling sign rose before us. The Town Line was as dump. A rusted sign, that was more of a design of carbon scars from a fire than a sign, hung over the building like the archway to a land of rust and ash.

We parked and walked into the Town Line's side door. On the faded blue carpet, I stood, looking over the worn light wooden railing down into the gray concrete floor where the green felt-covered billiard tables sat. I recognized a few people and the players who were good hoping the really good players were not there.

At that time, Tom and I were very good at playing the game of nine-ball. We would hustle games to make money. Our con went something like this: I would not walk in with Tom. We acted strangers. Then one of us would start up on a table. I would whack some balls around and lose. I would make a few tough shots, and it would seem as if I *thought* I were better than I was. Tom would challenge me and make delicate, precise misses. I would yawn and say such things as, "Good shot!" We would begin talking loudly of gambling.

Some nights no one played us. Generally, though, we got into a game of doubles. Best out of five. Whenever we began, I acted a great deal of frustration, holding my cue very erect, making the very easy shots, and missing the ones as I was supposed to. Tom followed up with a round of bad shots, and eventually, we would lose. This was the formula, for it was always followed by double or nothing. If the pineapples (the general term for our target players) were eager to stop, we finished it there with a run. We got the term *pineapples* from the way the fruit was used on baked ham. This made no sense, but made us laugh, so we used the word. I don't know who started it.

It was important to make it seem that our opponents almost won. That guaranteed another game. Most billiard players hate to lose after they've won and believe they can get back. The game Tom and I played worked most every time except when we ourselves were hustled.

The worst hustle done to us was the one by Fast Eric. He was as good a pool player as anyone I had ever seen. Tom and I backed him versus a player from Chicago named Platry Pete. We had watched Platry play, and by all rights, Fast Eric was better. It looked like easy money until Fast Eric began to miss and complain he was off and that he had not had a day this bad in months. When it was all finished, we were out eight hundred fifty dollars to Platry. Some months later, we learned Platry and Eric were partners and in Vegas.

Standing on the walk, I noticed my friend, a billiard player and hustler I knew as Zane. He saw me and called me over. He was at table 1, and he was smiling. He had a lit cigarette between his lips and was sitting on a table that had a game of nine-ball set in the rack. There was no smoking allowed on the billiard floor and no sitting on the tables allowed. I walked over to him. There were four high bar-style wooden chairs set parallel to the table and a small high-end table for drinks set in the corner of the wall. Two young attractive women were sitting by him. Zane was as gifted a billiard player as I had ever known and a few years older than I was. I sometimes played Zane to learn about the rolling of the cushions and about English and how one must use it in order to direct bank shots. For bank shots, there was no one better than Zane. He was almost supernatural.

Zane was smiling.

"No pineapples?" he asked.

"What?" I pretended not to understand.

"Suckers. Easy marks."

"No. No. Just here to relax."

He jumped down from his seat on the table and shook my hand. He had a firm handshake, and the best I can say, he resembled exactly the actor Robert Redford. Zane was much younger and wore his dark blond hair curly; but his face, his mouth, and his blue eyes were the same as the actor's. I once told Zane that he looked like him. He said he could not see it, but he would take my word for it.

Zane could outplay anyone in billiards but was very modest, especially toward other serious billiard players. Tonight he was stoned, his blue eyes red, and he had that steady restlessness of marijuana. The two women with him sat in the high-backed chairs, watching him play, and they seemed to be mannequins until one of them blinked. Then I understood they were scouting the other tables.

The first woman, named Juliet, had brown medium-length hair that was in tight-coiled curls. She had a sharp nose and was full lipped with gold-rimmed green eyes that shone a sort of wickedness. She had an exotic, muse-like quality one sometimes sees in a woman who is not traditionally, but is still, very attractive. The woman sitting beside her, named Lany, had platinum blond hair, which she wore long and straight down past her shoulders. She was much darker skinned, most likely suntanned, with a gentle smile in the corners of the mouth and silver-gray eyes that looked like Sandro Botticelli's goddess in *The Birth of Venus*. I remember hearing about these women, who were hustlers and very good billiard players, and Zane was mentoring them. Zane smiled with his blue eyes while racking, the balls clicking together.

"Game?" He offered his cue to me.

"No, thanks. I'll just watch," I said.

"It's all right. No wagers." He pulled out a wad of money. It was all crisp one-hundred-dollar bills. It was easily two thousand.

"I'd rather sit," I said.

"Suit yourself. If you'd rather sit, you would be at Jillian's. Have you been practicing?" He bent down, sited along his cue, and took a shot that was almost impossible. He made the shot, walked, and scouted for the next.

I stood, watching for a bit, then took a seat in a chair next to the women. They sat to my left. The wicked-eyed one was closer. I nodded to Zane. He had made another beautiful shot.

"And how are your bank shots?" he asked.

"Terrible."

"You don't need them."

"I'd like to make them like you do."

"Forget them. They are a deceit. They make beauty and looks. Like lipstick on a whore. That's all."

"They look great. You do them so well," I said.

"It's luck. I close my eyes and shoot. You'll see."

"I have no luck. I have to keep my eyes open."

"Yes, you do. You have luck. Plenty. This one likes you." He pointed at Juliet, the one with the curly brown hair.

"She is very pretty, no?" he asked. She ignored us. She was focused on a table nearby.

I looked at her. She looked either Spanish or French. I agreed. She was beautiful.

"She's my protégée, along with her friend, and she wants to jump you right there under the table," he said it, pointing, loud enough to get her attention.

I looked at her, and then I looked under the table.

Juliet turned and scowled and stuck her tongue out at Zane. It was pierced with a bar of silver. I watched the silver barbell move out and then back in to her mouth.

"He is a jerk," Lany added, speaking to me about Zane then turned to her friend Juliet. "We should get something to drink."

"She's at my loins all day." Zane motioned to his pants as if he were sore. "Please, Scott, take her."

Lany rolled her eyes then shook her head.

"Dog."

"Take her too." Zane pointed at Lany.

Juliet turned and scowled at Zane, shaking her head, then went back to surveying the nearby tables.

"I am a dog," Zane said magnanimously. "The young Scott, the old dog, and the two cats will be civil and will enjoy."

He was silent, I was uncomfortable—the women ignoring us, Zane perfectly happy, racking another game of nine-ball. He had sunk every ball in the first rack without missing. I watched him set the second rack. He was very stoned. He returned the triangle to the hold under the table and offered me the break. I declined, watching the same table Lany and Juliet were watching. It was a table of college-aged men who were playing a game of eight-ball, standing around drinking beer, laughing, and talking about gambling. Lany sighed and pulled her shoulders back, which thrust forth her breasts. They were round and very large and full. She sat posed like this.

Zane took his cue and bent, placing his left hand on the table, and stroked the cue back and forth with pivoting, his right forearm lining up the shot; then he held the tip by his fingers and leaned, snapping the cue forward. The cue ball hit with a crack, and the balls dispersed over the table. Zane stood and, when no balls fell, reprimanded his blond protégée.

"Why don't you just place your tits on their table?" he said.

"You mind your business." She hoisted her shoulders back farther.

"Those are my business." Zane reasoned. "You ruined my break."

"Such a pig dog." She kept her shoulders back.

"I need help with these two, Scott. Don't you see?" Zane leaned over the table and made a beautiful bank shot.

"Leave me out of it."

"Scott is a lover, not a fighter, ladies." Zane laughed loudly. "Scott is a lover! He is a pacifist!" He laughed, saying this very loud.

Both women turned quickly and looked at me, surprised. I think they thought he said masochist. I think that is what they believed he said.

"I would not let anyone tie me up," Juliet said.

"She lies. She was tied last night." Zane smiled.

"You're a stoned dog." The wicked eyes shot daggers.

"It's for my safety." Zane laughed more and indicated to me then shared louder. "They're too difficult."

Juliet looked at Lany and shook her head, but Lany was yawning and did not notice. She had relaxed her shoulders.

"That one has rabies," Zane whispered, pointing to Lany as she yawned.

I smiled but did not know what to say.

"If she has them, you're the one who gave them to her." Juliet rebuked and smiled as if she said something smart. She leaned over and whispered to me, "He's a dirty goat." Zane heard her and smiled, "A dirty goat that teaches you and gets you stoned and paid."

The wicked eyes flashed, and Juliet cursed at him words that I will not repeat.

"She's feisty." Zane shook his hands to me. "Take her, Scott."

"No. I'm all set, really." I tried to smile.

The wicked eyes glared at me.

"What's wrong with *me*?"

I must have blushed because she sat silent, staring and waiting for an answer.

"Be careful, Scott," Zane said, laughing more. "That old cat bites."

"Old? I'm seventeen, goat," Juliet said.

"Try twenty-one." Zane laughed.

I looked at her, and she looked very young. It must have been part of her hustle and con. She had bright skin, and her cheeks were fresh and pink and young.

"Nothing's wrong," I said, looking at her. "You're beautiful."

"Tell Scott your secret." Zane suggested to her. He made an obscene gesture with his hands.

"Go, hit your balls," she swore at him.

"Tell him. Tell Scott your secret against the years." Zane laughed, bent to the table, and made a shot. The cue ball sped and cracked off the ball he aimed for, then the nine-ball, sinking it.

"Slash!" Zane shouted, pointing with his cue and pushing another ball away with his hand. He came over to me and moved closer, pushing his face into my ear and whispered something about Juliet. It was dirty and made me choke. I tried to pretend I didn't hear it.

Juliet did hear it and seared her eyes at Zane. They were burning. I thought she was going to smack him, but she did not; and I think all of us, except Zane, blushed.

He continued, motioning to her, "Look at her. She's Dorian Gray herself."

Zane stood up straight and kissed the tips of his fingers, releasing them toward the air. "To the Art Spirit!"

"We haven't made any money, and I'm sick with this talk," Lany said.

"I'm not like that, Scott. He's a stoned pig goat. Let's go get a drink and have a smoke, Lany." Juliet motioned to her friend. She was ignoring Zane.

"Good idea. With my grass, you see?" Zane mocked. "Scott, where is the sanity? These two are imps. You want to smoke some grass, Scott?"

"No, thanks," I said.

"Grass is not good for young men in training." He smiled.

"Thank you, though." I nodded. Zane placed his cue against the wall and lit a cigarette from a pack on the chair. He inhaled then exhaled and looked at me, smiling.

"We are still on for Vegas?" he asked me.

"Yes." I nodded.

"We will make a killing."

"I would like that."

"You must practice every day. We will go in September."

"September is good."

"Is your phone the same?"

"Yes."

"I will call you. Do not forget. Practice every day this summer. Vegas in September."

"I will."

"Want the table?" He motioned toward his table.

"No, thanks, I'm going to sit with Tom."

"All right." He took a long drag on his cigarette and shook my hand. I felt very happy with him then and looked forward to our trip to Vegas. Lany said good-bye and walked away. Juliet smiled and touched my hand, telling me she really was a nice person and not to listen to Zane. She smiled, looking into my eyes, as she walked away. I watched her leave.

Zane followed and, not looking, almost knocked over a woman dressed in black who had just entered the Town Line from the side door. The woman stood, folding up a wet black lacy umbrella, and did not move when Zane approached. Zane looked at her apologetically, smiled, and moved aside. The woman in black smiled to him as if she knew him, but said nothing and just stood there, as if waiting. Zane turned and, leaning on the old wooden railing, shouted to me before he left.

"Keep this," he said, throwing me something. It was his chalk. I caught it. He always brought his own. "Do not forget to practice."

"I will practice." I nodded.

The woman in black was gone. I wondered if I had imagined her. Zane turned with a cigarette in his teeth, smiled, and exited. I thought of the Robert Redford and the Sundance Kid and Butch Cassidy and how much more Zane was a cowboy than a hustler. Always with that Zane con, that Zane smile, and his Zane way of life. He was the bank robber, risking and blowing it all up, using too much dynamite just to make sure the door came off. A few months later, after he killed himself smoking angel dust and jumping out a third-floor window, I tried to remember him as he was at the Town Line when we were going to Vegas and he was making his beautiful bank shots. He could not see the terrible odds that surrounded him. One thing or another surrounds us all, good or bad; but those we remember and love are the ones who laugh and keep going, storming out, fighting anyway.

AN APERITIF WITH MADAM FATE

> "[Zeus to Aphrodite:] Child, do you mean, by your sole self, to move unconquerable fate? . . . There a giant fabric forged of steel and bronze will meet your eyes, the archives of the world, that fear no crush of heaven, no lightning's wrath, nor any cataclysm, standing safe to all eternity. And there you'll find engraved on everlasting adamant the fortunes of your line."
>
> —Metamorphoses, 15.807-815

I heard footsteps in the rain.
Madam Fate—her manners gallant
With courtesy, refreshingly,
Her hand forward to kiss,
Adieu!—entered with her cards.

She sang,
May I sit?
By all means, please
Come out of that cold rain!
Warm. Dry. How do you do?

I am well.
Et tu?
How about a cup of tea?

Don't you just love dawn with
Her fingertips of rose?
She is so lovely, and now
I shall never want to lose this day.
Listen, hear those faint whisperings?
Those are the waking voices in the air.

They celebrate! The night is gone!
The night is gone!
Adieu! Adieu!
Zeus returned the stars

Upon their ether shelves,
And tucked the moon into its bed
And sent great Helios on his ride
So we see the world again!

I found in my hand strange set of cards.
They were large and engraved with runes.
What sort of magic is this?
The Madam dealt lithely.

Do not worry thee, the Madam sang,
I cannot deal badly, it is impossible.
Destiny wills thee from that wrong.
That is to say, that which are thy cards,
Are thy cards.

The cards, they found their hand.

The Madam sang in a mirthful voice,
Think thy are,
Thy are,
All that is thee,
In playing, be, therefore,
With thy heart see.

I looked at the markings upon the cards,
One card depicted three men lost in the desert,
One man dead, another collapsed, a third
Wandering toward a shattered visage,
A crumbled and gray ruin:
Here lies the King of Kings!
Look on it, mighty, and despair!
God is in the heart, not in the air,
Do not thy days as years.

I examined another glowing card's runes:
A bed of rock and stone
A house resting squat against a sandy coast—
And there upon the porch in garments
Loose and white,
Sat lovers by the day,
Blushing kisses on hot necks.

Another card sang:
Listen to those waters sing
Of proud Pangaean men
That hunt for stars
And camp in trees with wind.
Gnostics, all were lost.
That is no riddle.

And another card laughed:
If the Father,
And the Son,
And the Holy Ghost
Are one, then I am three?
Yet who walks behind me and in front?
Will a god or goddess tell?
Repent that!
You are one,
With lover, two—
Who is the third that lives among you?

Clotho, Lachesis, Atropos:
Moirae . . .

The Madam sang sagaciously,
The alchemists return,
So they say, to
Make gold of papyrus tea.
Drink Sencha tea to be free,

What?

Take thee. Take these that are thy cards.

I do not want them. What game is this?

It is thy game.

I do not wish to play.

Do you fear?

Yes. I do. I am alive.

Then come in, please, before Poseidon
Drowns you in the wine dark sea.

I am not Odysseus.
Nor Hamlet, nor Gandhi.
Nor president, nor prince.

Madam lit a long white cigarette and laughed.
To kill a man is pleasure.
To kill a song is murder.
Those are harlots singing in the lake, drowned a fortnight ago
In their escape. The men cry now, no more whores!
So go kill, all of you, all the same,
But for words, only different—
Take thy cards!
Take thy gun! But beware the bloody mud,
It jams thy gun.

Madam, please!
You confuse me!

Chasing things means nothing
And brings no joy.
Joy comes from honesty and tea.
So be honest with thyself
And have some tea.
Even though you will tell lies,
See that is not thy leaf.
Take thy cards.

No. I will not.

Then we must dine.
Have something in an aperitif,
French vermouth on the rocks, if you please.
Can you hear that?
Well done, maestro, your treatise—
He has done so well again!
Don't you think?

He was knighted?
He was killed.

The bloody mud.

"Vive La Vie!"
"Vive Les Dieux!"
Adieu! Adieu!

With moonlight in her black eyes,
The Madam danced and sang,
Please breathe, would you?
Your vocal fry does so annoy.
We only need anoint one's breath:
One part brandy, one part gin;
To release thee of thy sin.

Who are you? Good or Evil?
Why doesn't this light help?

Do not be offended, cried the wind.
The cards, they are yours and yours alone,
And what they say is for you—
The Madam finished many today!
We hear it in her glottal shock.

The Madam stretched and yawned,
Her straight black hair framed her
Pale face—she closed her eyes and smiled.
Free wind, go blow the dust!
Now you—
Thy entire are by breathing deep,
So breathe of thy deep breath!

Madam,
Stop! I cannot!

Thank me, darling, for thy tea.
How lovely, green, and tannic to the taste.
After dinner, shall I bring thee brandy for thy head?
Or more vermouth? Do not fret.

Madam,
I must go. I must find my love,

Your Penelope?
You mean, find thy death?
From sword to heart by sight,
A wound the doctors cannot heal,
The lover is the only cause and cure,

I must leave . . . she and I are expecting . . .

Do not fret about thy love,
Eat your baby,
Your firstborn,
Son of man, Man of Iron—
Beware, for Clay awakens soon!
Time is short, forget your love.
You have a life to dream before you wake.
Your cards are one.
You eat for two.
Don't love for three.
It is a blasphemy!

Madam, I quit.
Call me Job, and make me dust.

Thou art dust.

Please cure me of it then
And set me free
Kill me, as you did the rest.
I will not play.

You are full of life and drama!
Go on, you are full of fun!
Be quiet please and listen,
How I love Italian opera. Thank you!
Can you hear the old man singing?
His song is of the sea,
Of that Achaean who betrayed his duty for his pride
And sent the noble Hektor to his end.

Each man, right or wrong, takes his end.
The cards do not "mistell,"
You shall, as Ezra Mann did and does—
And we shall have an end.

How dare you, Madam!
Ezra Mann—why do you mention him?
How dare you!
You try to trick!

Adieu! Adieu!

She is mad, I tell you,
The wind moaned,
Bloody mad.

The Madam smiled and sang,
How articulate you are to say those things!
Perhaps you would like to be my song,
I like young rosy cheeks,
And have been so alone since . . .

I dare not.
Madam, I am done,
I work from morn to eve,
I feel my life to its top and breath,
And yet no gods or goddesses grant me
A reprieve.
I have been done in all along.
So I shall sleep and live.
Wake and drown.

Where has the Madam gone?
Madam? Madam? Am I alone?

One card lies untouched, it reads:
As the world is what it is,
Man creates folly,
Fear turns into god,
And all the world slips
Into a darker age.
Yet the stars shine behind the clouds and rain,

And the Madam dines with each
In her good time.

What is that sound?
Do you hear?

Yes.

It is footsteps in the rain.

BUILDINGS LIKE DOLL HOUSES

The woman took a long drink from her bottle of Corona. She held a set of tarot cards in one hand. She put them in her purse, looked at Scott sitting across the table from her, and smiled. The beer was cold and went down easy. She smiled with her eyes but stopped when a loud Harley-Davidson Road King drove by the street. Scott was sitting across the table from her. He spoke, "No other motorcycle sounds like a Harley, you know."

"Really?" Juliet asked as she placed her bottle on its napkin.

"You can fit pipes onto other bikes, but they don't sound the same as a Harley."

"I bet I can make the noise with my lips." She held two fingers up to her mouth.

"Seriously," Scott said, sitting back.

"I am serious." She made a trilling noise with her lips. "See?"

"Do you have to be so smart?"

"I am smart." She removed her fingers. "I made the noise, and earlier, I told you those buildings over there look like dollhouses. Wasn't that smart?"

"They are brownstones."

Juliet looked at the brownstones and sighed.

The two sat in front of Armani Café on Boston's Newbury Street. In the street, there was sun; so those people in cars or near the buildings were in the shade, the rest were in the raw of it. Iron tables with iron chairs and pink tablecloths stood angled on the sun-strained patio. Scott and Juliet sat in the sun, looking out onto the street. A waiter approached their table.

"Want to get another beer?" Scott asked, pointing to her almost-empty bottle. Juliet was biting her sunglasses.

"It is the kind of day to get a frozen drink," Juliet said, placing her sunglasses on the table. "How about margaritas?" she said.

"You make margaritas?" Scott asked. The waiter nodded.

"Yes, but we do not have frozen drinks."

"Pooh," said Juliet.
"We make margaritas on the rocks," the waiter indicated.
"On the rocks?" Scott asked Juliet.
Juliet fanned herself silently with her hand.
"On the rocks is fine," Scott finished.

The waiter brought out two margaritas on the rocks and two napkins. He put the napkins on the table and placed the margaritas on them, looking at Scott and Juliet, then went inside. Juliet's eyes were examining the brownstones. They were typical brick with tripartite design and concrete steps.
"They remind me of dollhouses," Juliet said.
"What?"
"Those buildings, they remind me of dollhouses."
"You know, they are brownstones," said Scott.
Another loud motorcycle passed in the street. On it rode a man in a silver helmet. The sun flashed in it.
Juliet covered her ears with her hands. Scott pointed.
"That's no Harley. See."
"It startled me." Juliet looked.
"It's an odd sound, don't you think?" Scott said.
"Look." Juliet presented her hands. They were shaking.
"You're too funny," Scott said, smiling.
"It was loud." She held her hands flat.
"How's your margarita?" Scott took a drink. The combination of Don Julio, Cointreau, and lime was hitting nicely; and he felt grand.
"Wonderful." Juliet sat back.
The hot sun glimmered on the cars.
"They make nice margaritas, right?" Scott asked.
"Completely exhilarating," Juliet agreed.
Scott was silent and then spoke, "I'm not saying you have to, Juliet."
Juliet fidgeted with her sunglasses.
"I'm not saying you have to at all."
Juliet remained silent and watched the shoes of the people walking by. Scott took a long drink of margarita. He spoke, "But we cannot be together like this."
"Do you think things will change if I do?" she said, sucking on the frame of her sunglasses.
"Of course they will." He reached and touched her arm.
"Really?"
She looked into his eyes.
"Yes." He sat back, looking away.
"Like before?"
"Of course, like before."

Juliet placed her sunglasses down, folding them shut next to her drink. She lifted her margarita into her hands and held it.

"Do you think you will be happy then?" she asked.

"What do you think?" Scott said sarcastically as he looked to the street.

"Please don't be cross."

"I am not," Scott lied.

"Will you be happy?" She fidgeted.

"Yes. Of course." He folded his arms.

She looked away to the buildings, wrinkling her wicked eyes.

"I'd like that."

"I love you, and I'm not leaving," Scott said.

"Even if I want to suntan and make noises and talk smart about dollhouses?"

Scott took a drink. "Yes."

"Or if I play pool or read tarot cards?"

"Yes."

Juliet hesitated and looked down.

"I just want you to be happy."

"Tell him, and we can be." Scott watched the traffic.

Juliet placed her drink on the table. She picked up her sunglasses then placed the edge in her teeth.

"Will you tell him?" Scott asked.

"Yes. I will tell him," Juliet said weakly.

"Will you tell him?"

"Yes."

Juliet leaned back, crossing her legs. There was no escape from the heat. She picked up her margarita silently, took another sip, and knew he was waiting for her to speak. She smiled.

"You really are my Romeo, aren't you? Well, Romeo, we could go to Cape Cod," she said. "To Cahoon Hollow and the Beachcomber and swim and eat like we did in June."

Scott took a drink, feeling the beads of condensed moisture on his glass.

"June?"

"You could get a lobster sandwich, and I could have the clambake. You could swim, and we could drink wine and walk and be in love."

"It's September."

"It's so hot. It feels like June."

"It's not."

"I wish it were June."

"No, you don't. Your ex was supposed to move out of your house and leave for Europe in June. He never did."

"Please don't get angry," Juliet pleaded. She paused for a moment then spoke with the hopeful energy of a new idea. "Let's get ice cream. I will call you my sweet prince and give you frozen kisses. I'm in the mood for soft serve with that berry dip that hardens."

"OK, I have to leave soon though." Scott looked at his watch then squinted his eyes into the sun.

"Don't be angry." Juliet took his hand. "I don't even want to think about your being angry."

She picked up her sunglasses and slid out her chair. Scott paid the waiter and then left a tip on the table; and together, they walked down Newbury Street, past the brownstones and the concrete facades.

"Maybe he will move out this month." Juliet skipped, watching her feet. "I don't even care."

Scott did not say anything.

"I wish I could make it all go away and just be what you want." She sighed. Scott looked at her and spoke,

"Move in with me. Then we wouldn't have to think about any of this."

She looked to the ground, avoiding his eyes.

"I don't want to talk about it anymore," she said. "I don't want to talk about it. Please. We'll sort it out, but just don't talk about it."

She walked and watched her feet and held Scott's hand.

"Just walk with me," she said.

She put her hand in his, and he held it as they walked.

At the ice cream parlor, a line of people extended up the stairs and out onto the hot sidewalk. "They're giving away free samples," someone in line said.

"How long is the wait?" Juliet asked a blond boy in the back of the line.

"I don't know. Ten minutes maybe."

Juliet wrinkled her eyes and thanked him.

"We better start to the train station." Scott pointed to his watch. "I've got class soon."

"All right."

Juliet and Scott walked arm in arm past Ciao Bella and Tea Lux, past the sunning tables and leaning umbrellas, places they had sat and spoken about this before. The margaritas wore off, and it was uncomfortable walking in the heat. They passed many brownstones, and Scott held her arm but got hot; so he took her hand. Her hand was shaking as if she were cold and shivering.

"Are you OK?" Scott asked. "What's wrong?" He kissed her hand and looked at her.

"I'm all right." Juliet said, looking at the street. "It's nothing."

AT SAN SEBASTIANO IN MANTUA

> For then thou canst not pass to Mantua,
> Where thou shalt live till we can find a time.
>
> —William Shakespeare, from Romeo and Juliet

I sit and listen to the jungle sounds
The spirits trapped in glass
Spin daily round and round.
The city sounds, a Mayan band,
Exist all o'er the city's peopled hand.

Rising flutes of varied breath chase voices
But the voices have no breath,
Or depth.

She speaks to me a sandy sacred din,
While days burn time to time we're in.

And what of love
For she and I,

Shall we dance in silk ambrosial shoes?
Or jest to be but tempted then to lose?

My heart, it screams.
It breaks and screams, and breaks and screams,
And breaks and screams,
And dreams,

As I sit and hear only the jungle sounds,
The spirits trapped in glass
Fall splashing to the ground.
Their shattered sound, their curling strands,
And love lost in fate's cruel falling sand.

THE WOMAN IN ROOM 29

She was a woman who lived with her boyfriend in a railroad-style apartment in Central Square, Cambridge, and she had taken the drug methamphetamine for sixty-four days straight. In the first twenty-one days, her friend Gertie, nicknamed Tea-Tree, had taken it with her. But after three weeks without stopping, Gertie quit—her friends having told her that the woman from Central Square was now most certainly a Krista, which is the worst kind of methamphetamine addict. So the woman had gone back to using the drug alone. It made the woman's boyfriend upset to see her each day with her thoughts only on the drug, and he always began dinner and prepared food and drink that were nourishing. The woman grew very thin and sallow, though still looked very beautiful and strong.

The woman was slim and curvy hips with small breasts and strong swimmer's legs. The small bit of light blond hair over her top lip glistened when she sweat, and it made her look odd under certain lights, either Greek or French. The light hairs ran down her whole body to her reedy arms and hands, but on her head was thick and full curly brown hair. She wore it to her shoulders, and her curls were natural and tight and as curly as coiled springs.

Everything about her was fading except her eyes that were the same color as emeralds, bright and burned gold around the edges and unguarded.

"Juliet," Jorge said to her as he placed a plate on the table for her and then a glass, "will you take Sally tonight? I have gotten my money from the restaurant."

"Yes," the woman said. "You don't need to."

"Remember that time we both took her and watched movies and made love for two days?"

"I remember." Juliet smiled. "I know you only stopped because of me."

"I could not breathe, and my heart began to pound," Jorge laughed, thinking. "Sometimes Sally takes me badly."

"I know," the woman said. "She takes everyone badly."

"Not you." Jorge smiled.

"I am a wicked girl," the woman said. "You do not have to."

"How is dinner?"

"It's yummy," Juliet said. She had pushed it around and had not eaten a thing.

"You're not hungry? You haven't been eating," Jorge said, now pushing his own food around. "I picked up new movie today. We can watch and make love."

"I would like that," the woman said. "I would like to make love."

They sat at the table, eating; and though the woman was not traditionally attractive, she was very attractive to Jorge who found her alluring and very desirable. Other women might look and think nothing of the woman, but it was because they missed her deep eyes, the swag of her legs, and the augur of her lips. Those who knew her spoke politely of her and said she was fine and well mannered. She had many friends, but those the woman kept had already married, and most of them had children. None of them suspected that the woman had a problem with drugs or did them daily. Those who used drugs themselves recreationally, either marijuana or some other, would never have suspected the woman. Her shoulders were always hoisted and firm, her eyes replete, and her voice pure and sound.

In the railroad-style apartment, Juliet divided the rent and utilities with her boyfriend Jorge such that he would pay the rent and she would pay food and utilities. When utility bills arrived for the apartment, she took them. For the last two and a half years, they managed that way except when they would go food shopping and sometimes would take turns. But one month ago, the January phone bill came, and there were charges on it for two hundred and sixty dollars to an 800 phone-sex number that made the woman confused and very angry.

"Jorge," the woman confronted him. She held the phone bill in her hand.

"Yes, Juliet?" Jorge asked. He was washing a plate in the sink.

"There are charges on this phone bill."

"For what?"

"Two hundred and sixty dollars." Juliet handed him the bill. Her hands were shaking.

"It is probably a mistake," he spoke, drying his hands on the white-and-green dishtowel.

He looked at the bill.

"The phone company always makes mistakes."

The woman looked over his shoulder. She was breathing shallow and fast.

"Yes. Just as I thought," he said, pointing to a line of numbers. "There's the mistake right there." The woman looked where his finger pointed then watched him speak, "Don't worry. I will call and take care of it."

She walked away.

In March, the woman cried all day after the phone bill arrived. It arrived on March 10, which was a Tuesday. There were 800 number charges on the bill for phone-sex. She, at once, broke up with Jorge. On March 22, there was snow, a storm that left ice thick in the trees and snow in the streets. The storm fell heavy. It was a long cold night, and they were still living together; and during that storm, Jorge apologized. After some arguing, the woman took him back. He begged her, promising never to do it again. And for a time, he did not.

On March 31, a heat wave hit New England, melting the snow, prematurely causing floods, the first time that had happened in twenty years. The phone bill arrived on the ninth day of April, which was a Thursday. The day after a pod of thunderstorms and tornadoes hit Jefferson, Alabama, where the woman's sister, Amanda, lived. The night before the tornadoes struck, Juliet had a vision about her sister. She knew she was in danger. But she hesitated. The only way to be sure was to use her tarot cards, in spite of the fact that she had promised to throw them away when she became a Christian. In her vision, her sister was screaming under a sky that was a murky green. Juliet was desperate. She dug out here cards and looked. Before she was done, she called her sister on the phone. While she was dialing, she thought about how terrible she was at being religious. With her sister on the phone, she warned her. Amanda, used to the accuracy of Juliet's predictions, listened and went down into the tornado shelter.

The next day in Jefferson, Alabama, tornadoes that struck killed thirty-three people. Amanda's neighbor's home was destroyed. Juliet called her sister many times to hear about how she was doing. She did not admit to anyone that she foresaw the storm or used her tarot cards. She instead threw them away as she was instructed and spent her time praying. She prayed for her sister and herself. Whenever she felt any intuitions coming, or any forewarnings, she confessed them to her church group. Those members told her things that made her terribly afraid of her "special abilities." When Juliet would cry and tell them she had visions, the group anointed her with oil in the sign of the cross. When Juliet admitted that she knew the tornadoes were going to hit, the church group fed her bread and Bible passages and urged her to be saved. No one knew of her drug use, though they sensed something within her that was not right. Juliet hid her feelings with terrible lies. But her church friends suspected something, and feeling worried for her, they drove Juliet to Cranes Beach in Ipswich, Massachusetts, at 7:00 AM on a Saturday and baptized her in the cold waters of the Atlantic.

At church, Juliet's soul was a graveyard. Her prayers were morbid. Her hopes were black. She devoted herself to learning the Bible, for learning seemed a clear way of acquiring that which she was missing. She enjoyed the church when it was empty, longing to see the corners filled with shadows and to hear the wind's moan through the stained-glass windows. The sadness in her soul mixed with the weariness she felt in her body, and all the days became desolate. She only felt normal on the drug, and when she was not on it, she would sink into despair. The church and its functions seemed more intense and more holy. She looked inside the cathedral and saw nothing but death. She began singing in the choir and devoted herself to helping new people learn about the church. The members enjoyed her piousness and taught her chants and prostrations. She ate them up like they were a warm wind ruffling over a meadow after a long winter's chill. She bewailed all the evil she had done. Would she be saved? Why hadn't she yet? She cursed herself for not being worthy. Could anyone love her? She did not feel the hands of the Creator holding her in his palms as she heard others say. She could feel none of the love or joy, none of the calm or piety, but only increasing regret that swelled within her. She tried to counter it with prayers on her knees and earnest suffering. But her spirit became all the more violent.

That night, on the phone with her sister, Juliet lied about the tarot cards and her visions and told her sister it was God that warned her. She begged Amanda to accept her Savior and receive eternal life. Amanda quieted her with thanks and told her she would. Juliet, however, could not stop using the drug methamphetamine and, in the deepest part of her, felt as if she were condemned to her evil life because she was born that way. If only she could fix someone else! If only she could believe as others believed! She gnashed and shook her fists to the sky, praying for salvation. But the angels did not come. Or the lightning. Or the thunder. The days with the drug began all over again. She knew in her heart that she was very sick for it.

When the first effect of the drug methamphetamine hit, it struck the neck from below the ears. The woman's blood burned, her shoulders and heart flashed hot and tensed, and she felt her every sense multiply. She was out dancing, and felt happy. She got lost in the bumping of hips, in the laughter, and in the music. The sounds of the nightclub opened in her, and she felt the energy in her legs and her breath and thought what a funny thing to think there were any problems. She was at the club Avalon on Lansdowne Street. She had grown thinner. Her face was paler, and her hands were shaking. Her tight curly hair, her long angled nose, her bright emerald and gold eyes all burned with a coldness as if she herself were cast from the ice of a glacier by some powerful magic spell. She had been seeing a nice boy named Scott who was from Gloucester. He promised to take her away from the fast-paced craziness of the city. Yet all her problems melted away under the spell of the music, and it was like the sea had rose and washed over everything and subsided, leaving nothing but the rippled and briny fun of the dancing. The Boston summer came and went, hot and balmy. A sense of ease came over her like a dark tan. Then she knew exactly what to do.

"I am moving out. I met a boy named Scott who loves me. I'll be moving out in October," the woman said with calm voice. She was taking off her dancing shoes. Jorge was waiting there when she walked in. "I found the man I can trust." Jorge watched her. She continued, "He loves me. He writes me poetry, and he is studying to be a doctor at Harvard. And I love him." Juliet sounded clearer and surer than she had ever had. It frightened Jorge—the resolve in her eyes, green and backlit by a light before unseen. She was deadly serious and calm.

"I am sorry, Juliet. I really am," Jorge said.

"Tell it to your whores." She walked into her room and slammed the door.

On August 12, the phone bill arrived. There were phone-sex charges on it for $255. This time, Juliet did not cry. She did nothing. She placed the bill in her purse and removed a small contact lens case. She swallowed down a bump of methamphetamine and, later that night, swallowed another. It was not working as strongly as it had, and she grew concerned. She contacted Disco Daffy, the code name for her dealer who scared her recently when he offered her syringes. She knew Disco Daffy, whose name was Dafydd, from Portland, Oregon; she had met him in 1994 while working at the Blue Ocean Art Gallery. Dafydd was a local painter and mathematician who liked to dance and Juliet would go with him to nightclubs around the city of Portland, Oregon. It was there that he introduced her to crystal methamphetamine. From her first time using the drug, she was hooked. She began using once or twice a month on weekends. This continued for almost a year, but in the winter of 1995, Dafydd was accepted to MIT in Cambridge, Massachusetts, to study mathematics. When he moved to Boston, it was not long until Juliet followed. In 1995, she drove across country to Boston. However, she could not find work, so she took anything she could get. Dafydd, meanwhile, though now selling the drug to make his rent, was successfully painting, having been befriended by some of the teaching staff at the Massachusetts College of Art. He told Juliet of an opening in the administration office. Juliet was interviewed and, in 1996, began working for the college.

Juliet visited Gertie on the night of August 12, high on Sally, with the phone bill in her hand. Gertie had quit using the drug and told Juliet she could not see her, that she was going to Narcotics Anonymous, and asked her to leave. Juliet, trembling, returned home. She confronted Jorge.

"Jorge," Juliet said, showing him the crumpled bill in her hand.

"Yes?" Jorge asked. He was washing his plate in the sink.

"There are charges on this bill."

"Charges?"

"Yes." She held up the bill.

He looked, drying his hands.

"Not 800 numbers?"

"Yes."

She handed him the bill.

"That's impossible. These have to be a mistake or something." He looked at the bill. "Look, these are old. They just haven't erased yet." He indicated, pointing to a line on the bill.

"You're lying."

"No. I'm not. I'm not lying. Get an old bill. You'll see."

She slapped him hard across the face, her eyes red and wet. "I drove you to them, didn't I?"

He stood there, motionless. Juliet tried to look at him but could not. She could not look no matter how hard she tried. She hit him again, breaking another slap across his ear that tore the silver chain from his neck. She fell to the floor, sobbing. Jorge followed her, apologizing.

The heavy white front door to the railroad-style apartment closed. A tall man with light skin and blond hair wearing a Red Sox jacket walked down the hall. It was Will. Will was enrolled as a student at Northeastern and worked with Jorge at the restaurant. He arrived to pick Jorge up for work.

Will shouted, "Hello!" and, walking, saw Jorge and Juliet on the kitchen floor. He turned away, averting his eyes, and apologized. Juliet noticed Will first; her eyes held him, and she did not move. Jorge jumped and yelled at Will, "Damn, man! Get out! I'm not going to work today!"

The night settled on the city with a cool wind. Juliet and Jorge moved into his bedroom. Juliet still loved him, but hated herself for it. She stopped kissing him, stood, and excused herself. She walked into the bathroom, closing the door. Her cat, Lórien, followed her and took a spot on the floor near Juliet's ankles. The cat rubbed its long whiskers back and forth against her foot. It was purring. Juliet pulled her hair in a ponytail and looked at herself in the mirror. Her eyes began to well up, but there was a noise by the door. It frightened her.

"I'll be right out," the woman said to the door. She heard a voice from the other side and then silence.

Juliet splashed her face with cold water and puckered her lips in the mirror. She hated her reflection. Such an ugly nose. She sighed, opened the medicine cabinet, and removed the lubricant. She raised a leg, placed her foot up on the toilet cover, and squeezed the slick liquid on her fingers. The wall of the bathroom was white; and she stared forward to the impasto *Road to Calvary* and the thick-painted Christ and remembered when she was in art class and purchased it cheaply and how it looked like a Cezanne. Once, there had been a painting of Zeus and Hera on the bathroom wall, painted when she was a young girl in Oregon and won an award for, but it came down when she became a Christian.

When she finished, she returned the tube to the medicine cabinet and proceeded to Jorge's bedroom.

"Where were you?" Jorge looked up. He was naked in the dark with the flickering television.

"My mother called."

"How is she?"

"She is well."

"Will she have us down for dinner soon?"

"Yes. She would like that very much."

Her mother did not call, and there would be no dinner. This was an invention they went through each time they made love. Juliet would tell it to cover her use of lubricant, and Jorge would believe and never question how very excited and very ready she was.

"This is a new movie I received in the mail today," he said, showing her the yellow-and-red video package. There were nude women on the cover censored with gray stars.

"What is it?" The woman sat next to him.

He showed her and read its title.

"That is very dirty." Juliet read the words from the box. They were words she spoke to him a hundred times in the dark. She wished each time she said them they would work magic and their incantation would charm him for good. She missed her tarot cards and cursed her wretchedness. She prayed to be a good person, yearned to understand love, and begged the stars to understand this man.

Juliet did not know if Jorge's receiving the mail was a fiction too, but it did not matter. She continued with the game as if it were real. She knew what he liked, and no one could be as good to him. She did what he wished even though it brought her no pleasure. She had long since felt any pleasure with him. It was the ghost of great love. She reached down and grabbed a bottle of wine.

"Should we drink some wine?"

"No, not tonight," Jorge said.

"Let's drink Dark and Stormies, like old times." he told her.

"Like the time we watched that nice film with Vivien Leigh and Marlon Brando?" she asked.

"Yes. What film was that?"

"*A Streetcar Named Desire*."

"I do not remember."

"I do, but we were very distracted."

"Who is Vivien Leigh?"

"She was also in the film *Gone with the Wind*."

"I haven't seen it."

"Yes, you have. We viewed it together, remember?"

"We did?"

"Yes. When I was at Amherst. We watched it in my room."
"Really?"
"I called you Rhett Butler, and my roommate, Susan, walked in."
"I remember."
"Am I not good to you?"
"Yes."
"And don't I do everything you like?"
"Yes."
"Remember the corset I wore when we took our vacation to St. Marten and we visited the Caribbean and you called me Bidane after that island woman prostitute who tried to seduce you on the beach."
"Yes. I remember. I remember the corset and the Caribbean."
"Do you remember when I went diving with the sharks, and you would not, and I told you about them and then the large bull shark?"
"I remember not feeling well and getting sick on the floor."
"From the tap water."
"Yes, from the tap water. And you did not get sick." He looked at her. "I drank the same water as you, and you did not get sick."
"I am a wicked woman. I do not know. Remember I told you I was warned not to touch the sharks as they swam, but I did anyway, and I told you how they felt like coarse satin and rough velvet sandpaper."
"You did."
"And the large bull shark that was the most beautiful and most terrifying and whose skin was the softest, and I touched him."
"You did."
"Kiss me."
She held her mouth to his, and they kissed in the dark under the flickering light of the television.

Juliet rose, gathered her clothes, walked, and shut the television. She looked at the room in the last snow light then pushed the switch, and all went to darkness. She rolled her clothes into a ball, went to the kitchen, and placed them in the gray-white hamper. It was very late, and the floor was cold; she did not think anyone would wake. But soon, Lórien, the cat, found her and began rubbing whiskers on her ankle. Soft whiskers pushed on her ankle in the darkness as the cat followed her into the bathroom. Juliet closed the door and looked at herself in the mirror, and the cat sat on its hinds and watched. It was purring loudly. Juliet began feeling very anxious, and to try to stop it, she washed her face.

In the dark, she took a new pair of underwear and her pajamas, put them on, and went to her bedroom. She did not sleep with Jorge because she rose early to work at the art college. She slept in the last room off the railroad-style hall and set her tiny mattress against the window. She fell asleep fast. At first she dreamed of driving in a car with her mother, the winding roads of Newport, her mother's home at Jamestown, the shale rocks, and the hammock she would lie in and look up at the stars. In the summertime, she would sleep outside and sleep deeply with the sound of waves, the cool seawater breeze, the high stars that were her friends, then the first light, bright and pink lemony yellow in the morning.

She noticed the lemony yellow light in her dream and heard nothing of her alarm clock; so she continued to dream and dreamed of Jamestown, the sound of the foghorns over the water, the gulls, and every night that was the breath of the day before. Then the sands solidified, the stars turned black, buildings rose, a city began, and all became alive with the noise of cars; and she was in Oregon. She smelled her old street and her old house, warm and rich: the old living room, playroom and the toys she shared with her sister, and her bedroom. Amanda was always doing something fun; her father in his office, quiet; and her mother in the backyard, gardening and feeding birds.

At twenty-eight, she dreamed about Oregon; but this last year, she stopped dreaming except about the ocean and her swimming in the Caribbean with the sharks. The ocean was vivid and blue, the sharks glided by her gray-and-blue silk with slow whips of their tales, and the glide of their fins quivered in the water. The sharks swam slowly, smoothly, and steadily from the blackness; and then the large bull shark came. Its eyes were black, its jaws open, and it glided toward her. Her vision filled with it as it circled until the alarm clock struck, and the sharks dispersed, the bull shark last, the water, the foghorns above echoed, and lighthouse spilled its flash onto the face of the deep. The woman stretched, yawned, and hurried to the shower in the dark of the early dawn, careful to be quiet.

Naked in front of the mirror in the bathroom, she stood by the white chair she had made in high school and began to comb her wet hair tenderly but stopped because of the flaw in her breast that made it smaller than the other. She hated her breasts and hated her legs too. She hated her legs and also her mouth for being too big. She would purse her lips and try to make her lips smaller, and she hated her reflection because it was very plain, unattractive, and not right. She looked at her finch breasts that were almost completely flat, with the one pitiful and flatter than the other. She hated them, and the smaller, she despised. She turned her legs and sighed. The only thing to do was to diet and not to eat and, if she did eat, to take a finger and vomit. She knew she could do this, not to eat or to eat lightly, and take Sally and use a finger once in a while.

The woman always told Jorge *te amo*, which is what the Spanish say when they are truly in love. She remembered when she first met Jorge—how clumsy he was, how cute, and his blushing while asking her to their first date. She had never been interested in him or ever thought of Madrid until sneaking into his dorm, looking at photographs of Spain and their first few months together, his showing her photographs of his family in Barcelona, and her remembering.

Jorge's college roommate, Eduardo, taught her the difference between *te caero* and *te amo*, which, is the difference between liking and loving. Juliet had never said love to anyone except her family and sister, and Jorge said *te caero*, which is what young children say for love. But when he made love to her, he called to her and said *te amo*, and she repeated it and believed it. He would whisper *te amo* while kissing her and making love to her and call her *divina*. She had never been called beautiful. Her father, who always wanted a boy but had two girls, treated her like she was a boy; and she played soccer though she really wanted to be a cheerleader. She dressed beautifully but disbelieved anyone who called her beautiful, though she hunted to hear it especially at night.

The next tornado that struck in Alabama was classified as an F5. It is the largest and most deadly size for a tornado. It was the only one of that size all year. Houses and roads that existed one day were gone the next. Juliet's sister Amanda's house was right under it.

In the small kitchen in Cambridge, in the railroad-style apartment, the cat, Lórien, walked over to his water bowl in the dark and lapped his tongue upon the water. Upon the table sat that month's bills, unopened, and in them was the phone bill. Lórien smelled his food bowl but did not eat. Instead, he walked slowly, turned, and walked toward his bed of blankets in the old wicker basket that lay under the table. He pressed it with his paw, gently a few times, then jumped onto it, curled his head on his front legs, closed his eyes, and went to sleep. Outside, it began to rain.

News of her sister reached Juliet, and she was shattered. She had ignored the visions and had long since thrown out her cards. Instead, she had been praying and spending time at the church. She held that month's phone bill that she had read before she received the call from her mother about Amanda. Juliet tore the phone bill up. She would not think of that or Jorge or anything. All that mattered was her sister and making that pain go away. She closed the door to her room and took a deep breath, trying to remember everything Dafydd had said. She prepared her arm and, after preparing the drug for injection, sat and cried. She cried and cried until she felt there was nothing left, and then cried more. The pain became so bad that she threw herself on her knees and prayed. But the pain swirling in her mind did not stop. And after some hesitation, she filled the syringe to the top with the drug and slid the needle in her arm.

It hurt, so she turned the pinch of the skin and squeezed. The burn, warmth, and smell of the drug filled her; and then it struck. She closed her eyes and exhaled. The blood rush made her arm drop the syringe, and she looked around her room as an unfamiliar place, down to the floor; then the ceiling lit oddly from the arched light coming in from the street. The apartment was silent, each room dark like an empty train stop in the city at night. She rolled out of consciousness and inhaled as if this had been the destination of a long journey that begun many years before to the expense of many hardships.

Lórien, the cat, came to her and sniffed his nose at the syringe and, forgetting it, rubbed himself on Juliet's ankle. Juliet did not feel the soft furry nose and ears. Vibrations of a purr issued from the cat's small feline engine. It sat on its haunches, licked the skin of her foot, and pushed his white whiskers into her dropped hand.

Juliet, rolling then falling then swirling, passed through a dark and shadowed forest. Overhead was much obscurity, the trees were very dense, and in the breaks between the boughs, she saw a starless sky. Behind her she heard strange sounds, as if the breathing of a dog. She looked back and in the darkness saw a creature that seemed at once a great she-wolf, though it had the mane of a lion and wore spots as one would see on a leopard. The animal frightened her, and she turned to run. She ran until she came to a large gate set in the center of a towering stone wall. There she stood before the gate, looking at the latch, old and rusted, lit in the dark by a cold and pale light. She halted there and, from that place, remembered every destination she ever visited, missed, and searched for a way back with great longing.

Then she heard it or, more rightly, felt it. She screamed and looked. It was a voice. A voice emanated from the gate! It grumbled ominous and troubled like a giant creature growling and gurgling in its throat. Juliet could feel the voice inside her bones. It sent out a shockwave throughout the very air. The iron bars of the gate bent and flexed. Its voice sounded of doom.

"I am the way that runs among the lost. The way to desolation. Abandon every hope, who enter here." Juliet became hysterical. She screamed and turned to flee, but she was met by a figure. She held her breath and crouched, watching the movement and rustle coming toward her with terror. It was a cloaked figure of a woman, very familiar, yet unknown. The form appeared silhouetted in the darkness, adorned in black, and spoke strange words to Juliet; and Juliet began to cry. The woman wore a black dress and black hat, and with a black umbrella in one hand, held her arms open. It was her sister Amanda! Juliet ran to her, threw her arms around her, and hugged and squeezed her, crying. From deep within her belly, in the place where she breathed, Juliet cried what felt the rush of the entire ocean.

Juliet was back in her room upon her bed, the soft light of the street lamp slicing to the floor by way of the window. She pushed and pushed against the rushing ocean and pushed and began sobbing. She heard Zeus in his starry heaven shaking thunder and felt the dust of the stars in her soul, and the way became clear.

She took a deep breath and, closing her eyes, descended in search of Amanda. She walked and walked until at last she came across a dark figure. It was a young man, with an athletic body, and winged sandals, broad-brimmed hat, and wooden staff. Seeing her, he smiled. He held out his hands. Inside, Juliet knew everything would be fine. He told her soothing things and took her hand; together, they approached the groaning gate.

The dark swelled around, and the light dimmed until Juliet noticed the lemony yellow light recede and saw nothing. But far away, she saw her mother's Jamestown and heard the sound of the foghorns over the water, the gulls, and the night, breathing for the following day. And then all congealed, the light curved, and she heard a city. She remembered it and smiled at all the buildings. But she could not find her house, and so called for her sister, Amanda; but Amanda was not there, and no one came except the ocean and the sharks.

The man holding her hand vanished. The city sank down and the ocean rose up in a swell of endless water. The flooding occurred quickly until all the city disappeared beneath the cold dark sea. There was nothing but silence. The first shark glided past her and then a second and a third—gray-and-blue silk with slow whips of their tails, the quiver of water, and the glide of their fins. The sharks circled slowly around her, and she could not breathe, but it did not matter. Then slowly from the blackness, the large bull shark came. Its eyes were black and its jaws open, and it came for her. Juliet reached her hand out, felt its long sleek body, and grabbed to hold its tail. It circled with its jaws open, and the water and all light faded from the deep in the early light of Cambridge. The bull shark swam; and the woman held on to its dorsal fin and, holding tight, drifted away with it into the deep dark of the abyss.

In the railroad-style apartment in Cambridge, it was Scott who found Juliet first and called the ambulance. Earlier that day, he found a message on his phone from Juliet. She was crying hysterically. Between sobs, she told him that her sister was killed, that she never meant to lie to him. She cried about being addicted to meth amphetamine, and that she was sorry, that she would take care of everything. The last thing she said was she was going to find her sister. Scott went crazy. He rushed to her house. He called the phone repeatedly, but no one answered. He broke the door down. He ran up the stairs. He did not care if Jorge was home. To hell with Jorge. Scott was in love to the ends of his being; and when he found Juliet, he gasped—had not seen anything like it, ever, and it broke him inside. He swore at the world, picking her up and gently stroking her hair. He called the police, the fire department, an ambulance—all, while he held her in his arms, crying, with his head rested on her forehead. When Jorge arrived and saw the front door broken down, he stormed in, shouting. Scott met him with a punch square to the jaw. Later, as Scott walked to his car, he was still crying though no one could tell because of the rain. It continued raining as the fire trucks and ambulance sped away with the police following. The rain washed over the streets as Scott's car followed under the clouds into the gloom.

THE SIGHS OF THE SUN

Since I wronged you, I have never liked you.

—Spanish Proverb

I

The room is set—a soft light overhead:
Two voices,
A symphonic minuet
Of sighing notes.

"What is that sound?" she asked, sitting cross-legged upon the ground.
"Infandum renovare dolorem."

In the faint moonlight of lost hours,
Standing gray obsidian,
Talking in my evening coat, I say,
"I cannot stay,
But thank you for the tea."
Beneath the music quivering, she sips,
"I see autumn is coming.
Green and red and yellow in the trees."
My eyes have known these, living in New England,
These sighs of the sun.
But in that lamplight,
Under that fading lamplight,
Under afternoons, her soft hands,
The evening swoons,
I
Should say, "I remember us in spring last May,
You in your sundress driving to Cape Cod."

Recalling these October nights,
"Perhaps you would be so good to write.
For everybody hoped, as I . . ."

II

In the pavilion,
The windings of broken violins at sea,
While slowly twisting, drown—
She slowly twists her fingers round while speaking,
"Be well won't you and write.
I always keep contact with each I've loved."
But what have I to say?
"I will remember your address. And if ever you
Would like . . ."

I cannot what I would say,
But then she speaks,

III

Upon the terrace,
Under frozen Greek facades,
Remarking rhapsodies,
"How lovely Boston is."
Pretending these October nights
Are Gershwin fantasies,
Stoppard travesties,

"How pleasant is the fall."

IV

There in the hall,
Upon the velvet divan she remarks,
"You do not understand and
I wish you could see.
How wonderful, he, it . . .
My life . . . is . . ."

My expression jumping from the dock,
To the hymn of a coronach.
"But I have no regrets.
And am sure
There are things I won't forget."

Yet what have I to say?

My eyes then stray
Slowly to the floor,
As if searching there
For something hidden or rolled
Behind the door;
Then turning slowly on the latch,
I turn and say, "Adieu."

"Adieu, amoure, adieu."

THE WASTE LAND

In the cold part of the evening, I was in my living room, curled up on the floor with a blanket, watching reruns on television, sipping tea, wondering if it were true. I watched the television in disbelief. The country was going to war again. In the street beyond my window, ice held cold and hard, and the sky was dark and gray. I took out the rabbit's foot and looked at it. It was worn and smooth where the fur had rubbed off. I remembered Ezra cutting the lucky foot and then burying the rabbit in the cemetery in Revere all those years before. That was so long ago, it seemed another life. I put the rabbit's foot back in the pouch in my pocket that also held a small worn piece of green billiard chalk and a small shriveled-up starfish set in clear plastic. Ezra was gone in the last war, and here we were starting another one. I took a drink of tea. Maybe Ezra would meet Juliet, and together, they would find Zane and see the Rose under the sun of endless spring. I thought about them all, wishing it different, and in a rush, remembered each death that did not seem real. What had happened? I wanted answers. I wanted to hear it was a mistake.

 Juliet Ariadne had been dead for four years. It was all a nightmare and a vicious dream. Despite the time that passed, I still grieved. Why did it have to be her? We could have been married with kids. What was it that I could not see? Why was I so blind? I did not want the mystery. I loved her, but I was very angry. I looked at my hands. They had been useless. I felt my heart. That was useless too. I could not save her, though I tried, I tried more than anything I had ever done. I thought about it, and it made me ache a terrible hollow inside.

 Zane Crescenzo had been dead for eleven years now. I thought about Zane, smiling, and his humor and how he would be very upset that I stopped practicing and never made it to Vegas. He would probably tell me life is too short to miss anything and not to wait for him. He, with his beautiful bank shots that were a sort of magic and playing better than everyone. Of course, I stopped practicing after they found him dead. I lost my desire to play billiards. I even convinced Juliet when she was alive that billiards was a waste, and she stopped playing too.

Ezra Mann had been dead now for fourteen years and four months. He was one of those killed in the first Gulf War in an out-of-combat accident. Ezra was killed when his S-3B Viking crashed shortly after takeoff during a routine mission in the Persian Gulf. A thirty-six-hour search involving ships from the Gulf War battle group failed to turn up his body. He was my best friend in the whole world. He could make me laugh just by walking into a room. I thought about fighting in the Middle East and of the war starting now. Some people weren't made for wars. Ezra had a good soul. He died serving this country, and that is very noble. I felt he did us all a great honor, and it was then that I realized that patriotism is really about valuing the country as a family, and Ezra died protecting his. I watched the television some more. The United States and its allies were invading Iraq. The fighting in that region over the centuries had taken its toll. Much of it was a waste. But wastelands are everywhere, not just the desert. If the king is wounded and needs healing, we see it in the land. No amount of arm or armor, politician or politics will fix it. Perceval must be allowed to work. At 11:00 AM on November 11, 1918, an armistice was signed that was supposed to be the end of all war on this planet. It was to be the beginning of a new age, an enlightened age, where humanity recognized war was hell and nothing is solved by a fight. I wondered if any of those men who wrote and signed that Versailles Treaty were drunk when they did. We all love, lose, live, and die—we are all brothers and gods wherever we all live. And the earth calls us all back the same. I looked outside again, and it was dark, and a storm swelled in the clouds.

In the street beyond, ice held firm and cold, and the sky was bleak and gray. I took a drink and thought about the summers at Ezra's house, by his pool, with his family sitting under mosquito nets on warm nights under a clear sky. I looked up at the Gloucester sky. In spots were thin, swift clouds, beyond them the black sky with bright stars. I heard the long-drawn report from the Coast Guard station's foghorn echo over the house and heard a snowplow crashing over the street. It continued down by the yacht club, down toward the Coast Guard station and the Dog Bar, its steel shovel breaking the ice, its wheels cracking it to pieces in places.

The trees were covered with black ice, their leaves long fallen, and the plows crunched the ice by the trees near the street. Under the sky, the trees were dark without their leaves, the streets black, and the ice on the streets, cracked and white.

Some time during the night, the snowplows sanded and salted the road. The city dispatched a battalion of trucks and machines resembling large steel elephants, salt falling from a cold steel pipes like dung. Large wheels caked and rolled over ice, slowly underneath, the behemoths pushed on. Smaller flat bed trucks with many lights roved with concave plows angled like a scowl, and these tore the asphalt as they broke pieces of ice and snow from the road.

There were strong winds that blew the hills white, making the trees fluffy white and leaning. Those winds made snowdrifts in the roads and brought out the elephants that thundered by, the drivers guiding them like zookeepers, having an impossible time even if they drove all night. Sometimes I would take a walk out to see the night, but in the storm, it was too bad.

That winter was cold in New England, but the days were usually sunny; and in the morning, through the windows, the sun felt warm. Gloucester streets are tight with houses, and there are many tucked in along the sides and beside them the harbor and river. There are always a few vessels in the water, and that year, boats went out for lobsters. In some mornings, I would watch them from my deck, which overlooked the Dog Bar and the inner harbor, though the boats grew less and less.

Far away from where I was in Eastern Point, beyond the bridge spanning the Annisquam River, lay the railroad tracks and farther the Highway 128. There were always cars on the 128, even during snowstorms. Their lights bright in the dark. In the warm season, it was a scenic ride as it looped by the ocean in Beverly Farms and hooked inland past large camps of trees when they were alive and thick with green leaves. In winter, Route 128 was dangerous because of the black ice. The road froze to black and shone polished except for the green and white signs, yellow signs, and orange signs. The highway's low banks, edged with trees or gullies, were filled with frozen water or dirt sprayed on mounds of snow—and the road too, which sometimes hardened to ice.

In the spring, there was a fog over the roads and the harbor. Cars would fathom it with high beams, the March snows collecting on their side mirrors while birds cried ghostly in the mists. One day in April, as the rain fell, it turned to snow and collected in large flakes, crystallized—white thickening and melting on the asphalt, downy in the grass, which made my old cat, Lórien, shiver and shake funny as though dancing.

In October, I moved to Eastern Point; and by Christmas, we had snow; and by January, the ice came. But it did not hold for too long, and by the end of March, the snows had turned to rain.

II

My father said something to me years ago that has always stuck in my mind. It was a bit of advice. "Son, forget what everyone else is doing, just make a living at what makes you happy." Turning to that advice repeatedly through my mind, after undergrad college at Harvard and preparing for medical school, I decided I should be a writer.

To begin the switch, I came to settle in Gloucester. Gloucester is a very beautiful, very historic town that is very rich if you have money and even richer if you are poor. That year, I was very poor, though that was no different from any other year. I was attending Harvard Medical School and not working, I needed money. So I began house-sitting for a Dr. John Fischer. He owned a lovely house at the end of the road in Eastern Point that sat among the yacht club, the Coast Guard station, and the lighthouse. The view was of Gloucester's inner harbor, and then beyond, the Atlantic to Salem, and on to city of Boston, thirty nautical miles due south. I commuted to and from Harvard in Cambridge, Massachusetts, on the train. To make money, I got into the Internet. I read all the books I could find on it and, soon after, began consulting for a financial firm. When the company went public, I did really well. All of a sudden, I earned a lot of money. I think that was the problem that happened with Juliet. I imagined that I had enough money to take care of her and all her problems. If only she moved in and lived with me. I could fix everything. And what I could not fix I could pay for or buy. I could make everything OK. I could take care of her. I soon learned money does little good for relationships. Still, after she died, so did my being well-to-do. The Web bubble burst. Everything went down. The money vanished.

I took what capital I managed to get out and used it to live while in school. Even with a full grant, living was still very expensive. It was during my first year at medical school that I began writing. I wrote a screenplay for a film about an accident-prone man working in a fashionable café in Boston. He would wear the wrong shoes and would trip and fall. The crowds, who wore Armani and drank very expensive martinis, were unsympathetic; and it was a comedy. I imagined him as a sort of Buster Keaton who reacted to it all with a straight face. I sat, imagining the man spilling a tray of drinks on a woman as she rose to answer her cell phone. It was then that my phone rang. It was Dr. Fischer.

"The wife and I are going to Rome. We need someone to watch the house in Gloucester until the spring. You interested?"

I moved to Gloucester in September. I had just enough money left to live if I did not have to pay rent.

Gloucester turned out different than I had hoped: the streets, the people, and most of the surroundings were very friendly. There is a sort of camaraderie in that town that encourages artists and, most likely, comes from years living rather richly and rather desperately at the same time. Something like too much fishing and not enough fish—they were strong people. But there was still much tension from the massive shrinking of its fishing industry.

My first night in Gloucester, I dreamed I would never fall in love again; and after I moved into the house on Eastern Point, it was easy to see how that might happen. I never went out. I commuted to school and came back again at night. I was so busy with school; I lived very simply—studying, drinking tea, commuting. How does anyone who commutes have a social life? I wondered. Can you *live*? Really live with a long commute? I hoped it would change when I became a doctor. Every day I wrote in a journal. And every day I wrote of being unhappy.

My father, a self-made businessman who was in construction, started his own construction company in Boston when he was nineteen. People called him Gus, but his full name was Aegeus; and if anyone made fun of his name, he punched them in the nose. He grew up in an old half-Greek, half-Italian neighborhood in Boston where he got noticed for being a good pool player. Then his uncle Pandion, nicknamed Pan, who was what Hollywood would call a tough guy, went partners and got my father started in the construction business. My uncle knew the business and taught my father, and when I was a kid, my dad would take me with him to the supplies shop where all the local construction people met. On the weekends, he would take my little brother and me out with his friends.

"You hungry? You want to eat?" We were always eating, always hungry, and would play Sinatra when we drove in Cadillacs; and we always went to dinner before we saw a movie. My father loved the movies and would talk about the actors as if they were his personal friends. "Robert Shaw is a good guy. Why can't a shark eat that cog sucker at the city hall?" He would talk about any present enemy.

The day after the movie *Jaws* came out, my father took my brother and me to the beach. He was hoping to see someone eaten by a shark. "Get out of the water!" he joked. He was the kind of person who would swim under you and grab your leg. You scream, and he thought it was the funniest thing in the world. "Hey, how 'bout Roy Schneider tossing that chum and the f—shark's head pops up. That little f—Richard Dreyfuss. I wish the f—shark ate him. Him and his f—glasses and that Jew voice. That Spielberg did a good f—job. He's a Jew too. That's the f—racket to get in. That's f—Hollywood. Listen to me, Scotty. Movies."

So while studying to be a doctor, but I wrote to keep the Hollywood idea alive. I moved to Gloucester with those words echoing in my mind. While on the train, going back and forth to Harvard, I wrote a script for a movie about a man, a hero, who journeys to the underworld like Odysseus and battles Persephone and Hades to save his lost love. It was a retelling of the Orpheus's myth meeting the labyrinth of Daedalus and was where I was at the time.

Dr. Fischer's house was a beautiful home squeezed in between Gloucester's Coast Guard station and Eastern Point Yacht Club. The view overlooked the Dog Bar in Gloucester Harbor where the sky was always vivid and high, and the bushes between my house and the yacht club's were thick and overgrown.

My aunt Augustina and uncle Virgilio also lived in Gloucester, near the high school. I spent whatever time I could in their house, which was little, in those days. I was very busy. I would call on the phone my *tia* (the Italian word for aunt), and she would always invite me over for dinner. Tia and Virgilio's house was lively and very loud. Their front door was never opened, but the door around the side always was; and inside, it was warm and inviting.

I would drive there and park in her driveway that was almost part of her yard. I could see the lights behind the shades and hear voices, talking and laughing, and I was happy when they invited me over to eat because I rarely had home-cooked food.

My tia was directly from Italy, moved to America twenty years before while my uncle was trying to make something of himself and was venturing in the restaurant business. My uncle was my mother's brother, and he opened a small restaurant on Main Street in Gloucester where above the entrance he had a motto engraved in Latin, *Venite ad me, omne qui stomacho laboratis, et ego restaurabo vos*, or "Come to me, anybody whose stomach groans, and I will restore you." In the summer, he served pizza, cold beer, scampi, and icy cold white wine. In the winter, homemade lobster raviolis and veal, pork simmered in a hearty red tomato sauce with deep red wine, and garlic on soft bread. And sometimes he did so well his tables were full with people, and when it was slow, my uncle would stroke his chin and think about a new coat of paint or decoration of flowers for the windows. At heart, he was a gardener.

In the beginning of autumn, after I moved to Gloucester, I was down and having a hard time. I became depressed. It came over me one morning, started as a bit of doubt; and then everything was trouble and anxiety, and my days were filled with shadows—darkness fell over everything, and suddenly I was exhausted. I slept all my free time away and could not eat. My mood went past irritable and angry, past unhappiness, and settled somewhere below an evanescence of miserable. My ideas were tired, and there were dirty dishes piled in my sink.

After many weeks sleeping, drowning myself in sleep, and sleeping through entire days when I was not at school, I watched the sun set over the ocean, from the top of Tia's hill, in their driveway beside the hedge. I stood, sipping green tea out of a large cup. Henry Fielding said tea was the panacea for everything, "from weariness to a cold to a murder." I smiled. Tea was one of my favorite things. And during those days when I was depressed, I would easily pick tea over some people. I knew I could rely on it and nothing could ruin it but bad water. My uncle crunched on a red apple as he readied his garden for the coming winter, and I watched the sunset. Looking at its orange and pink colors on the river, I knew I just had to stop thinking, to let go and move on. I just had to focus on today. Finishing school. Graduating. There was no use hanging on the past.

My uncle walked over to the trash and threw his apple core away as my friend Keri pulled up in her convertible. It was warm, so she had the top down. She looked at the driveway, waved at me, and pulled her car in past my feet. She was smiling. Earlier, I had called her and invited her to dinner at my tia's, and she was very happy she came. She got out and was full of smiles, and we hugged. Keri Maiara was one of my best friends at the time. She was in college, studying oil painting, and had just left her fiancé of nine years; and we would console each other. My uncle noticed her, said hello, and stood with us for a while. Tia came out to the porch and called us to dinner.

That evening, my tia made seafood Fra Diavolo, a legendary dish of hers that was over spiral macaroni and mixed with garlic and hot peppers; and we ate slowly for she always made enough—sliding our bread through the red sauce, sprinkling cheese, talking loudly, laughing, drinking glasses of a Tuscan Chianti that was dark and tangy, which slid down slightly ahead of itself and made our belly warm. After pushing our plates away, my tia began, as usual, talking with Keri.

Keri was a quiet woman with beautiful large, pale gray eyes like a cat. She was about 5'5" and wore long brown hair straight down her back. Her pedigree was Native American. Her grandmother was a noted Ojibwe who kept her family's native history alive by teaching it at a local community college. Her grandmother claimed to have actual letters from French traders dated from the 1700s. My tia spoke always in Italian; but when I was there, she talked English to me and always talked English to Keri, who would blush if she did not understand, though sometimes Tia forgot and spoke Italian anyway.

"Keri, you and Scott go out?" Tia asked, looking at both of us. She said half in Italian; so Keri looked at me, confused, having caught her name and mine, and blushed. This was a topic my tia was always on.

"You don't like him?" Tia asked her. "You and Scott go out?"

"Yes." Keri hesitated. "No."

"You don't like him?" My tia proceeded. "Keri never liked him." She was explaining this to my uncle. Tia was up now, holding the large spoon that stirred the sauce; then to her satisfaction, she scooped out a steaming heap of scallop and spooned it on my plate, smiling at me all the while, keeping Keri in her attention.

"Keri doesn't like Scott. She drives all the way up here to eat." We all laughed. "She doesn't like him! She drives all the way up here to eat!" Tia spread out her hands and laughed with us. Keri laughed, and we all laughed more.

"Being depressed is usually caused by malnutrition." My uncle theologized, his hands folded on his large belly. He was looking at me. He was an after-dinner scholar. "I read that depression comes from having too many bad irons in the fire, and you can offset this with food. Supplements from algae or sea moss, I've heard."

"Did you ever read *The Baron in the Trees*?" my cousin Marco asked. "I love that book. I will let you borrow mine. It's about a boy who lives in trees."

"That's a stupid book." My Tia interrupted. "Who lives in a tree?"

"Mama!" Marco yelled over his shoulder. "It's a story! A metaphor! It's good." He reassured me. I thanked him. "Don't listen to him." Tia whispered, gesturing circles with her hands. "He is crazy. How can you live in a tree?"

"You should buy that book," Marco instructed me.

"Intelligence isn't always a feather in one's cap: the smarter one is, the more likely one's wits are to fly the coop." My uncle belched as he read his magazine. He sounded like Jack Nicholson, whom he greatly resembled. "Your problem is you're too smart, and you trick yourself."

"If you're smart, you don't eat algae. Read Calvino," Marco whispered to me then said in a louder voice, "You go eat seaweed in your garden, you crazy old man!" The back door opened, and my younger cousin Carmine strolled in. He was whistling a song. I felt the cold night air rush along the floor from behind him.

"It feels like there will be snow," he said.

"No." My uncle emitted a low rumble. "The forewarned are forearmed. It will only rain." He turned to Keri. "You can still go dancing."

"He's a weatherman now," Tia exclaimed, making fun of my uncle who belched again.

"You should go into the city with Keri," Marco coached me. "There is a bookstore in Newbury Street, I forget the name. You could pick up the Calvino book."

"Eat, drink, and be merry, for tomorrow we die." My uncle took Keri's hand. "But tonight, go dancing."

"You should go to the bookstore. It's in Newbury Street."

"You can go to cousin Mark's. He's having a party." Carmine hummed, looking in the refrigerator. "I saw him today."

"Business before pleasure, Carmine." Uncle embogued. "And Mark's apartment is too small for dancing. Look at Keri—she was made to dance. Don't waste the night sitting around Mark's. Carpe diem!"

"Mark needs to find a nice woman," Tia said, taking a gulp of her wine. "Someone to get him out of that stuffy apartment. Scott too." She waved her wooden spoon at me. "Keri just comes up to eat!" Tia screamed loudly, put the spoon down, extended her arms, and held my face with her hands. Her palms were rough and warm. She got closer. "So handsome! You don't need her." She waved Keri away. "You find a nice girl." She laughed.

"These are the salad days. I would go dancing now if I were you're age." My uncle evacuated.

"If you were going to the bookstore, I'd ask to go. I love the city's bookstores. Especially Newbury Street," Marco said.

"There will only be rain. Keep your sangfroid. Drive slow."

"Stop by Newbury Street, and if you are hungry, have an order of the sweet potato fries."

"They won't be hungry. Paint the town red!"

"Who's hungry?" My Tia looked at me, astonished. "You're hungry!"

"He's not hungry."

"Calvino is the author's name."

"How many angels can dance on the head of a pin?" Uncle waxed. "Don't forget to spin her, Scott!"

"You ready?" Keri asked. My family was as loud as ever. Keri came close and spoke to me quietly. "We should leave if we want to park. I'll have to drive slow if it rains. My tires are bald, so I hope it doesn't rain. I hate driving in the rain."

"You're hungry? Eat!" Tia said, putting a plate down in front of me. It was full of pasta, steaming.

"No, thank you, really, Tia, I'm full. I am. I must go. I'll eat it later."

"I'll save it for you."

"Thank you so much."

"Thank you," Keri said, hugging Tia.

"You give me a kiss." Tia smiled at me, and we kissed and hugged. "And you too." She kissed Keri.

"You come tomorrow. I'm cooking."

"I will. Thank you, Tia!"

"Ciao, ciao!"

"Good-bye," I said.

"Good-bye," Keri said too.

AN ODE TO AUDREY WILDE

Where is your bliss? Not in things
To be counted, no, that is a waste. Land lies
Where the sun beats, there beside the water—
Listen to the water, crashing on the rocks.

When I returned, late, from our walk on the beach,
My arms full, my hair wet, you could not
Help kissing me the first time we met,
My eyes fixed there upon the water in yours.

That day you set a hundred tears,
Neither blue nor red nor green,
Fine art by Audrey Wilde,
Lady of the rocks, wooing her Prufrock.

It is the autumn in a week or two
The season marking the fall,
But my mind as new as when I was
First in love, with the moon and stars in you.

THE SIAMESE FIGHTING FISH

A man and a woman drive in a car down a winding Cape Cod road. They are on vacation. It is Saturday, and dusk has just begun. The man is Scott Theseus. He left medical school to pursue a career as a screenwriter. The woman is Audrey Wilde, Boston artist. She works as a bartender and is trying to quit working and return to art college to teach. Scott holds his left hand, which is bleeding. He has it wrapped with a blood-stained dishtowel. Audrey is driving. They speed along in Scott's aged dark green convertible Saab. They are both in their thirties. Both are attractive. Scott fits the stereotype for tall, dark, and handsome, though not in a rugged way, being more like a dancer. Audrey, with her long, straight brown hair, light skin, and blue eyes, though not traditional, is exotic looking, her origin most likely being French. The two are very close, that is apparent. They have a connection that allows them to use a sort of empathy with each other. This night, however, they are visibly stressed and agitated. They have been fighting (which they have been doing more and more of), and it has left them both silent. Each wears a tired exasperation like a scarf. They have moments of revulsion at their own weakness, yet they will not betray each other. Audrey cannot stand that Scott dropped out of Harvard Medical School. Her father, though successful, was an alcoholic who died of drinking and left the family broke and in debt. Seeing a lack of money as the obstacle to every kind of happiness, Audrey feels very justified in seeking comfort through financial stability. Doctors do not starve, artists do, and she is proof of that. Scott has taken this very personally. He believes, if she loves him, she should stand by him, whatever he decides to do. Who, being loved, is poor? He often asks her. During the last fight, which began during dinner, it was revealed that Audrey's best friend, Emily, thinks because Scott dropped out of medical school, Audrey should leave him. Scott lost his temper and threw his wine glass and dish from dinner table. They shattered on the wall. Reaching out to clean them up, he cut his hand badly on the glass. Now they speed in the car to take Scott to the hospital in Falmouth, Massachusetts, for stitches.

SCOTT. This is fun.
AUDREY. What? (*Continuing to drive, speaking, but not looking at him.*)
SCOTT. This. All of this.
AUDREY. Don't start, darling. I was enjoying the scenery.
SCOTT. I am the one bleeding. It's easy for you.
AUDREY. I am driving you. Be a sport.
SCOTT. I'm bleeding on something. What are these? Country music CDs?
AUDREY. Oh, darling, no! Don't bleed on my CDs!

The October day was mostly gone, leaving a harsh and penetrating chill. The soft breezes of the summer were giving way to brisker winds. The failing flower beds and empty gardens, like an old person, seemed to give themselves up to age. The sky turned gray, and the wind was changing to the east. The evening was approaching, blurring the outlines of the houses and trees. Nothing was in the air except a thin dust and the occasional gray-specked bird high up in the sky. The dust thickened the air. The yellow grasses of the dunes waved in the changing wind as the car passed. Scott and Audrey sped down the road like dust through a dried-up damn.

SCOTT. I am sorry, really, I meant no offense to your country music or Keith Urban. (*He holds up a handful of CDs with his good hand and puts them on the back seat.*)
AUDREY. Be a nice chap, and don't bleed on Travis Tritt. Oh! And watch it, that's George Strait!
SCOTT. You know what's funny? This is my car.
AUDREY. So?
SCOTT. I don't listen to country music! I don't even have a CD player!
AUDREY. I took my portable, darling. Would you like to hear something?
SCOTT. I thought you had an iPod?
AUDREY. I do. Well, I did.
SCOTT. You did. The little green one, right?
AUDREY. It was so small I accidentally washed it in the washing machine, darling.
SCOTT. Oh.
AUDREY. Don't worry, we have plenty of music and this old CD player of mine works just fine. I have some Van Halen. I know you like them.
SCOTT. Yep. It always goes back to Van Halen. The country's gotta go though.
AUDREY. Be a sport! I'd much rather you handsome than sarcastic.
SCOTT. Can you believe this? (*He holds up his wounded hand.*) My wonderful temper.
AUDREY. You have a tiger's temper, darling.
SCOTT. Rather I was a teddy bear.

AUDREY. It is too bad, really. You made such a lovely dinner. And what was that delicious French wine? Pity I only had a taste.
SCOTT. You thought the food was good?
AUDREY. I always like when you cook, darling. You're so cute when you do. It's what I was saying, you are much too handsome to act a lunatic.
SCOTT. I should have at least tasted the potatoes. I slaved over them.
AUDREY. Don't you know me by now? Getting angry and throwing things. It makes for a bad game. Why do you insist on treating me like other women? Are you trying to be funny or something?
SCOTT. Not really.
AUDREY. You are funny, you know. You were laughing when you threw your plate. And that wine glass was cheap. What did you expect? Cheap glass is always the most wicked when it breaks. Is your hand very bad?
SCOTT. Those wine glasses were cheap. Damn that *Target*, I will never shop there again.

The wind blew strong, and the houses along the streets leaned on it. Dust blew into the trees along the streets onto the asphalt and into the grass. Hundreds of small birds, chirping and whistling, moved in the wind past the rooftops of the houses. They moved as one, as a school of fish does under the water—up, then down, then turning sharply. High above, the lone hawk, spent from a day of hunting, vanished into the windy sky; and the smaller birds formed long queues along the telephone wires.

AUDREY. I will sing to you, if you want.
SCOTT. No, no. Let me. (*He begins singing the Van Halen song*, Hot for Teacher.) "I think of all the education that I've missed. But then my homework was never quite like this!"
AUDREY, *laughing*. You are a wonderful singer, darling! Oh, it is so terribly out of tune!
SCOTT. Yep. I am one notch above horrible at least. You always said you liked my singing. Said it made you feel like you could sing anything.
AUDREY. It certainly does. Oh dear, I think I just ran a red light.
SCOTT. You will be arrested for sure. I would turn you in, but this is my car. (*Looking at her.*) So what happens after the hospital?
AUDREY. I am not sure, darling. We could have sex.
SCOTT. Oh sure, change the subject. I mean about what you said. What your friend Emily said about you leaving me.
AUDREY. Let's not talk about it, darling, be a good sport. I am sorry I said it. I shouldn't have said it. We are on vacation. It is my fault really. I really shouldn't have said it.
SCOTT. I don't mean to start, but it got me worried. I am your friend. It is better to tell me how you feel than keep it bottled up.

AUDREY. The way you cooked and slaved over those potatoes was so charming. I shouldn't have said anything.

AUDREY. We should have got stoned before dinner.
SCOTT. I didn't know you had grass.
AUDREY. I don't. I meant drunk.
SCOTT. I wouldn't anyway. Grass makes me feel claustrophobic.
AUDREY. You get claustrophobic anyway, darling. Remember when we were planning to go scuba diving? You got claustrophobic in the store while trying on the wet suits. We are on vacation, we should have some fun, relax. All this has put too much stress on us, darling.
SCOTT. I agree.
AUDREY. Tell me that love poem you recite for me. Be my Prufrock.
SCOTT, *pausing*. OK, but first, I want to officially apologize. I am sorry, Audrey. For frightening you. You are right. We should not fight. It ruins everything. There is nothing to win.
AUDREY. You called me a gold digger, darling. How funny is that?

The car passed, raising the dust off the road, which carried in the air and then settled. Dogs were barking in the distance. The dust blew into the trees, the grasses, and on the roads and darkened the sky. High up, it tinted the clouds gray. Along the sides of the road, dust landed quiet around small piles of leaves that littered the gutters with motion then with stillness.

SCOTT. I didn't mean you. I meant Emily. What Emily is saying is all about money. Listen, screenwriting is my dream. I dropped out of medical school to follow that dream. As an artist yourself, I know you understand. It does not have anything to do with wanting to be poor.
AUDREY. Yes, darling, I understand. I will love you whatever you do. I do understand. But why can't you do both? Many doctors write. Look at Michael Crichton.
SCOTT. You are right.
AUDREY. I think you are very brave darling, and I respect you for being brave.
SCOTT. I want to be good to you and spoil you. We will be the most fun married couple. You will teach art, and I'll write. We will go to the beach and swim under the sun and drink ice-cold white French wine.
AUDREY. How is your hand? Is that the hand you write with? No?
SCOTT. No. It's not the hand I write with. It's all right.

The dusk sky turned a deep gray and red, and distant large, white-gray clouds rose up like mountains in the horizon, ethereal and looming. Some of the clouds gathered as if in formation of a storm. Others sped away and opened up the deep sky. All about the winds and the clouds moved. The enormous sky stretched and yawned thunder, and the winds pressed over the dirt into the trees as if a giant had loosed them from an invisible cage deep within the earth.

SCOTT. I am hungry.
AUDREY. Me too, darling. And to think, you did a great job with those potatoes. The meat loaf too.
SCOTT. You think?
AUDREY. Yes. Absolutely.
SCOTT. You're not just saying that? You wouldn't be the first person to pass up a plate of my meat loaf.

SCOTT. Meat loaf is an art form I . . . (*holding up a package of cigarettes*)
SCOTT. Are these cigarettes?
AUDREY. Give me those, darling.
SCOTT. Are these yours?
AUDREY. Are those cigarettes? Well, look at that. Be a good sport. Give them here.
SCOTT. You told me you quit six months ago!
AUDREY, *taking the pack from him*. So how do you make that meat loaf, darling? Do tell, please! Be my darling Prufrock, and tell me.
SCOTT. Forget the meat loaf. Cigarettes?
AUDREY. I cannot forget the meat loaf, I loved it.
SCOTT. Are they yours?
AUDREY. No. Not really. They are Emily's.

The air was thick and the sky thin, and the setting sun made it more thin until it became night. The wind blew up and all around. Birds on the telephone lines sang against it and, then in one great leap, took to the sky as a single movement. They flew away, and the night greeted people returning home after long hours of working. Men and women embraced, wiping off the dust, kissing, turning on porch lights. In the glow from the windows, folks ate dinner, leaning forward, talking. The wind, dust, and clouds filled the sky as day became less and the night, more.

SCOTT. When was Emily in my car?
AUDREY. Oh, last week, some time, darling, you know how I like to borrow the convertible and drive with the top down.
SCOTT. I had it cleaned before we came to Cape Cod.
AUDREY. Oh, then maybe one of the cleaners left them.
SCOTT. I had the outside cleaned. I cleaned the inside myself.
AUDREY. Well, darling, that is the last time you should take it to that place then! Be a good sport. Stop asking.
SCOTT. No doubt. (*He examines his hand.*)
AUDREY. How is your hand?

SCOTT. So what else?
AUDREY. What do you mean?
SCOTT. What else do you have to tell me?
AUDREY. I adored your potatoes.
SCOTT, *laughing*. I mean, what else? The fight we had at dinner started over Emily.
AUDREY. Darling, listen to me, I do not smoke. I just occasionally do. Emily cares about me, she knows once in a while I like to have one. A woman's entitled to what she wants.
SCOTT. So you don't smoke, but you do.
AUDREY. Yes.
SCOTT. And this makes sense.
AUDREY. Perfect sense. Yes.
SCOTT, *looking at the speedometer*. OK. So I guess if you get pulled over right now you, you could tell the officer, yes, I was speeding, but I wasn't speeding. Or if you were to sell one of your paintings, you can tell them it's $1,500 and it's $2,000.
AUDREY. Please be a sport and stop.
SCOTT. I think you get this attitude working at that bar. The people come in and want a drink, but they don't. They do twelve shots, but they can't remember.
AUDREY. Darling, are you through? You are very funny, but really, do you care if I have a cigarette?
SCOTT. I guess I care, and I don't care.
AUDREY. Good, because I would like to have one now.
SCOTT. There they are. Be my guest.
AUDREY. You sure you don't mind, darling? It is your car.
SCOTT. It is. But I don't mind. What's mine is yours. Besides, I am bleeding all over my car, and it is filled with your country music CDs, what's a little smoke?
AUDREY. Do you have the lighter that was with them?
SCOTT. Here (*hands her the disposable lighter*).
AUDREY. I'll be a sport and roll the window down. See? You know, I wanted you to make lasagna! Imagine what a mess that would have been!
SCOTT. I like your lasagna better than mine.
AUDREY, *lighting a cigarette and taking a deep drag*. What do you mean?
SCOTT. I wouldn't have thrown the lasagna if you made it. I would have eaten it. If we fought, I would have thrown something else—your fish tank, I suppose.
AUDREY. You would not! She is just a little innocent fish!
SCOTT. That innocent fish tore the fins off the other fish we put in there, remember?
AUDREY. She is a lady, darling, she demands her privacy. Want a drag?
SCOTT. No. Thanks. I have to watch the asthma.

AUDREY. I'm kidding. I know, darling. Be a good sport. My window is down. See?
SCOTT. You can forget kissing me now.
AUDREY. I wasn't going to kiss you.
SCOTT. Is the hospital nearby?
AUDREY. Almost.
SCOTT. Give me a kiss anyway.

A harsh wind filled the sky, filled with dust and chill. It blew down to the houses, down the road, pushing on through the trees. People arriving home late shivered in it. Rushed fires sprang to life under chimneys. Furnaces burned and headed against it. Drafts snuck through the door cracks and windows. Blankets were taken out. Chocolates, teas, and brandies were heated and served. Above the sky, blackened and seared, the dusts swirled; and the clouds growled with thunder.

AUDREY. Now that I am done with my cigarette, I am going to sing. (*She flicked the butt out the window and began looking for a CD.*)
SCOTT, *speaking with his eyes closed.* They are all in the backseat. I did not accidentally throw some of those country CDs out the window.
AUDREY. Don't you dare, darling! It is time for some good old country singing!
SCOTT, *looking, watching the streets, and noticing a pet store on the corner.* Hey! Isn't that the pet store where you bought the travel tank for your fish?
AUDREY, *singing along with the music loudly.* Yes!
SCOTT, *yelling to be heard above the music.* She is a Japanese fighting fish, right?
AUDREY. Siamese. (*She continues singing.*)
SCOTT. Siamese. Right. You know, my cat, Lórien, tries to eat her.
AUDREY. What? (*The music is too loud.*)
SCOTT. Nothing.
AUDREY. You don't want to sing along, darling?
SCOTT. I think you are the only woman who brings a fish on vacation.
AUDREY. Are you saying you want me to stop singing, darling?
SCOTT. No. I am talking about your fighting fish.
AUDREY. I know you are sorry for throwing the dish, now be a good sport, sing!
SCOTT. Yes.
AUDREY. Sing!
Scott tries to sing but does not know any words so just hums.
AUDREY. Are you singing, darling? (*Laughing.*)
SCOTT. Yes. (*Laughing.*)
AUDREY. I like it. (*She laughs.*)

The windows of the houses lit with small golden lamps like stars in the darkened night. Dogs barked less and less in the shadowy yards, each returned to warmth, nuzzling to their masters. Houses hummed quietly, each a mystery of its human engine—grand containers of the cogs and wheels and springs of family life—vibrating with that contented din that comes from being a home. The cold dust sped in the wind, thickened by the sobering rain, and set earth upon everything.

AUDREY. Oh damn! I missed the turn! Hold on.
SCOTT. U-turn? OK. (*He holds on with his good hand.*)
AUDREY. Watch your hand, darling (*turning the car around*).
SCOTT. You really are a horrible driver.
AUDREY. I am. Your car does not like me. She is jealous of me or something.
SCOTT. She is nervous you will crash her into a wall.
AUDREY. I was singing and forgot to drive. (*She turns the music down.*)
SCOTT. So this is the right way now?
AUDREY. Yes.
SCOTT. So it really scares you, me leaving school.
AUDREY. Yes.
SCOTT. Is it because doctors make money, and there is no guarantee a screenwriter will make any?
AUDREY. It is not just that, darling. It's just, to do art and be paid, it takes years. Sometimes you never get paid. Sometimes ten to fifteen to twenty years maybe, if you're lucky. You see me at that bar working like a slave. I slave for them. My art is solid and unique and good, and yet I slave for my rent. I slave to buy food and clothes. I slave to keep a car. I am sick of all the slavery, darling, and of eating meat loaf, you know?
SCOTT. So the truth comes out—it *was* the meat loaf!
AUDREY. I love your meat loaf, I didn't lie (*laughing*). No, no, you are a gourmet, darling, but truthfully, I am sick of the game that has no show. I am sick of renting and missing sunny days and of ramen noodles.
SCOTT. You eat ramen noodles?
AUDREY. No. Never.
SCOTT. So are those like the cigarettes? You don't eat them but you do?
AUDREY. No, I never eat them. I mean, it's complicated. Be a sport, darling. I am sick of struggling. I am sick of working just to have a tiny bit of time to paint. I want to live. I want to love the game. I want to make art and teach and have babies. Lots of babies. I want summers off to tan my legs and only worry about getting sand in the car or whether my white capris will show off my tanned legs, and enjoy the aperitif I am having.
SCOTT. I am going to take a job while I write.
AUDREY. You know what I mean, darling.
SCOTT. I like everything you said. I don't look good in capris though…

AUDREY. You are very funny, darling.
SCOTT. Being a doctor is not my only safe bet.
AUDREY. You are fantastic at everything you do. Anything you do is a safe bet. I do love what you write.
SCOTT. Thank you.
AUDREY. I have been painting since I was a little girl. I have only ever been paid for nine pieces and two installations.
SCOTT. You are a hell of a painter too.
AUDREY. You know what I am saying. How many rejection letters do you have from your short stories?
SCOTT. Enough to decorate a holiday tree.
AUDREY. That is all I am saying, darling.
SCOTT. Well, I know I am following my dreams. All of them. And even if I make the wrong decision, I will still give you my everything. You say art does not pay, but what about love?
AUDREY. I am not happy being poor anymore. But I am in love with you. (*She begins looking around.*)
SCOTT. What are you looking for?
AUDREY. Another cigarette.
SCOTT. You chain-smoke?
AUDREY. No. Hospitals make me nervous.
SCOTT. Really? Is it my hand? I can cover it better. Look . . .
AUDREY. It is not you, darling. Hospitals remind me of my father. Oh!
SCOTT. What?
AUDREY. I cannot breathe!
SCOTT. You can't breathe? How about stopping smoking?
AUDREY, *hyperventilating*. I think I am having an anxiety attack (*looking at him*). I am sorry, Scott, it is not you. (*She stops the car.*)
SCOTT, *taking her hand with his good hand*. Relax. You do not have to go in. Drop me off.
AUDREY. No. No. I am OK. (*She lights a cigarette and smokes, her hand visibly shaking.*) It's all part of the game. I'm all right. How is your hand?
SCOTT. It hurts. I will need stitches. Did you bring anything to drink?
AUDREY. Yes. There's a bottle of water.
SCOTT, *handing her a small bottle of water*. Relax. Take a napkin and dab some on your face.
AUDREY. Thank you, darling. (*She takes a long drink from the bottle then puts her head back and begins dabbing her neck and forehead with a napkin.*) So, darling, something funny, have I told you some of my friends think you are shy?
SCOTT. No. Some people think that though.
AUDREY, *laughing*. It is true, darling! They do.
SCOTT. Is it because I am the strong, silent type?

AUDREY. No, darling, remember when we first got together, how you never touched me, never even came near me for a month? You would not even kiss me!
SCOTT. That was the dead giveaway? Are these the same friends who drink cosmos from oversized martini glasses and think their lives are the lost episodes of *Sex in the City*?
AUDREY. Well, why didn't you try to kiss me, darling? I have always been curious. You had not seen me since we were children. Didn't you think I was beautiful?
SCOTT. Seriously?
AUDREY. Yes, darling. Seriously. Be a sport, and tell me.
SCOTT. Seriously, Audrey, I felt . . . I felt that if I touched you, if I got too close to you, I would disappear.
AUDREY. What do you mean, disappear?
SCOTT. That is exactly what I mean. I mean I would disappear.
AUDREY. I had to jump at you to get a kiss, darling.
SCOTT. It was the greatest kiss of my life.
AUDREY. I love kissing you, darling. Shame on you for making me wait. I cannot imagine life without kissing you. I would go crazy from missing it.
SCOTT. Did Emily say that to talk bad about me?
AUDREY. No.
SCOTT. But you guys were definitely smoking something stronger than cigarettes.
AUDREY. OK, so you are not shy?
SCOTT, *pulling something out of his pocket. It was a starfish, dried and withered, set in a piece of clear hollow hard plastic. One of the points of the star was broken.* This is the starfish you gave me when we were kids on the beach. I keep it and carry it everywhere. Truth is, I have been in love with you since I met you. And every day I feel it more. I didn't want to kiss you if you didn't love me. That would have killed me, and I would die and just disappear.
AUDREY. *throwing her cigarette out the window, she touches the starfish, looks at Scott, and then kisses him. When the kiss concludes, she pulls slowly away, smiling, and starts to sing.*) Sing with me! (*Audrey turns the CD player on.*)
SCOTT. Will you sing to me in the emergency room?
AUDREY. I will. Once you are checked in, we will sing a duet, darling.
SCOTT. Who? David Lee Roth and Sammy Hagar? I cannot do Sammy Hagar.
AUDREY. OK then, how about the Starland Vocal Band, darling? We can sing *Afternoon Delight*!
SCOTT. I can certainly embarrass myself trying.

THE LIGHTS OF THE CITY

The lights of the city remind
Me, could I forget?
There is so much—
Extra—empty beside me.

Voices in the glowing dark
Under hot paper porch lights
Fill the gapped night air,
But one voice is missing.

Windows shape the night
Filled with fare and laughter.
I see days in old pictures,
They are the light's home now.

I still remember when
That candle was first lit,
And there were pink and blue clouds
Bursting castles in the rain.

The same waters that
Fell then, fall now.
But they do not fill
Emptiness, or wash missing away.

AT THE MAD FISH

I found the waitress and raised my finger. It was a young brown-eyed woman who walked over, smiling. I ordered another Corona with lime and another chicken casadia. She walked away, and I turned the napkin over and continued. I was supposed to meet a client for work at the Garden of Eden restaurant in Beverly, but they canceled, so I got in my car and drove to East Gloucester instead to work on my career as a writer. I was trying to lighten the mood of it and write while thinking of that.

I was writing on a napkin. It had been a year since I dropped out of medical school to get started as a writer. I was making no money and was under a great deal of stress from that. I could not sell anything writing and was working for myself as a personal trainer. Audrey Wilde and I broke up; and I sat there, scribbling on the napkin, trying to get my disillusioned feelings out. She was an artist. I was an artist. We both enjoyed Cezanne. We could dance well and kiss well, and I knew she was the one for me. The truth was I fell in love with her when I was nine years old, at Nahant Beach, down near the Tides Restaurant. My life had never been the same. But life has a way of covering the shiniest things with dust. The dust erodes everything, even rock—what chance does the human heart have?

Audrey went back to college. I heard she had taken a job as an assistant art teacher. She was back in college after many years and I was happy for her. But I missed her every day. This day I had not said that yet. But I knew it was only a matter of time.

After I left medical school with no money saved and no money coming in from writing, I needed to do something, so I started a company consulting as a physical therapist. I got all my clients via word of mouth, got them into the gym, and taught them about eating better. I just encouraged using organic foods, focusing dishes around protein and healthy fats, and exercising four days a week, even if it's a half-hour walk outside. For most people, this would be very helpful. But my business was slow. So I went to the Sunny Day Café in Gloucester to write. But I discovered the Sunny Day Café had been knocked down and rebuilt into a new restaurant, which I did not care for. The change killed the magic that was there and now it was a bistro, and bistros are terrible places to write. So I drove down to the artist colony in East Gloucester, to a place called the Mad Fish, which was a restaurant that had a nice deck overlooking the water. On a sunny day, in the summer, it was as good as any a place in the world to write.

I sat there on the deck of the Mad Fish in the sun. I wrote a few paragraphs, then drank the rest of my beer down and chewed on the end of the pen for a few moments and then began writing again. I was working on a short story but got distracted by the sun and began a letter to Audrey that became a piece of masterful fiction. I was using a short stack of napkins.

"Hey, Scotty! Good to see you here!" I heard a woman's voice. I raised my brow and looked. It was Christina. She and I had had a date, but she stood me up. Charming gal. Since Audrey, I have had no luck with women. Christina was the bartender, and she wore a big smile, talking to me from behind the bar. I liked her because in the dark, her blue eyes seemed gray pools of great depth that reflected messages of the words that you said. Yet under the bright light of day, Christina's eyes took on a bright sharp powder blue.

"I am so sorry about the other night," she continued. "You know how things come up. I meant to meet you. I hope we still can get together," she spoke rather abstractly. She was very busy with work, yet she had a patented way of speaking, possessing the ability to say nothing and convey nothing, yet articulate a meaning. I called it the articulation of articulation. I watched her speak and thought about Audrey. Damn you, Audrey.

Christina continued, "I didn't hear from you during the week, and until I read your e-mail, I did not think that we were still on. I didn't get your phone call till late, so I didn't know and felt really bad about missing you." I smiled at her, took a deep breath, and put my pen down—this being much more interesting than what I had been writing.

"Did you see our new cheese wheel? It's over there." Christina pointed to a large wheel of various cheeses set out on a table. "It's spectacular, and the Brie is great."

"I haven't even seen it. I didn't know," I said. If only I thought like that, cheese would fix my world. I laughed to myself, what do I know? Nothing at all. Apparently, life is sometimes extraordinarily funny, and you just cannot tell—maybe cheese does help, like they say chocolate does, or drinking. And when you feel you cannot live one more breath and Madam Fate has dealt you the worst hand, have some cheese. There is nothing better.

My laughing to myself was not helping the awkwardness of the situation, as my writing was probably not helping the general state of literature; and even if this beautiful woman apologized ten more times or if the cheese wheel was as spectacular and as festive as a holiday, she had done me wrong. And I knew from that moment on, she could never like me. She could not, from that moment on, be honest. It's a funny thing, the way that goes. When you do something bad to someone, you immediately stop liking them, even if you try. It's as if seeing for the first time your poor behavior and reproach yourself for it, promising to do better to the next by first destroying the errors of the past.

The server brought a Corona, and I lifted the lime wedge from the bottle and squeezed it until it dripped out its juice and then pushed it down into the neck and took a drink. It was cold and refreshing and slightly ahead of itself. I looked back at the bar. Christina was serving a group of three seated men, making stories with her eyes. It seems all bartenders have the unique ability to convey ideas and anecdotes with their eyes. Maybe it is in the job description.

I was feeling grand drinking the beer and enjoying the deck, the sun and its reflection in the water and the boats and watching the people in their boat shoes hanging out on the docks. The Mad Fish sat on the south side of the small inlet that did not, at all, reminded me of Spoerry's Port Grimaud in France, a place that I visited during the summer of my sophomore year in college. I took a bite of the casadia and, while chewing the hot melted cheese and soft corn flour and feeling grand, decided to flourish the truth. I grabbed a napkin and wrote Christina a letter.

"To be honest, I do not think it would work for many reasons, my being in love still with my Audrey Wilde, but mostly, my dislike of cheese." I laughed aloud, looked up, and was distracted watching an attractive woman walk in and sit at the bar. She was with a man. They were together and obviously in love. I knew it because they were breathing for each other's smiles. Just then, I could feel it coming back, the swell in my throat, but I would not say it. It swelled in my blood, and I felt dizzy and disconnected. On the radio, a Van Halen song played, the lyrics getting into everything,

> *I wrote a letter*
> *And told her these words*
> *That meant a lot to me*
> *I never sent it*

I looked out over the water, at the sunlight, to the trees against the far shore. Damn it. Damn it, Audrey. Damn it all. I will not say it any more.

I looked back toward the woman sitting with the man. She wore a long straight brown hair, and the man had curly, almost-stringy hair. The woman reminded me of Audrey, but the man reminded me nothing of myself. I heard the man speak in a gruff, slummy voice, "That was so stupid. I can't believe how stupid that was."

I tried to listen more but could not understand, so I returned to my casadia. Christina, with her beautiful smile who stood me up, came to mind as if inside there had been a television clicking on. I remembered I had seen her at the Sidewalk Bazaar on Saturday, the day we were supposed to go out. She was there, standing with a group of others, smiling in the sun. She lied. I laughed and wrote on the napkin, "The Sidewalk Bazaar on Main Street was fun." I crumpled the napkin. My terrible luck was biting me again, and I was sick of it. I wondered about my lucky rabbit's foot. Since leaving medical school, nothing has been easy. Why did I? Why not just finish, do what everyone wanted me to do? I would probably still be with Audrey. "Be a good sport," she told me so many times. It broke me to thousand pieces to think about it. I had to stop. The answer was obvious. I will have some cheese. I laughed.

I was feeling very alone and stretched back in my chair. Christina walked out from behind her bar and over to me, her gorgeous smile leading the way. She pulled up a chair and sat with me at my table. She looked beautiful, and the Corona was helping.

"Want another? It's on me."

"No, thank you," I replied. "You don't have to."

"I forgot to tell you, that day I got caught up in plans, I already had to help my friend move. She and I went to the Sidewalk Bazaar to find her a few tapestries for her new apartment. I meant to call you, and then everything got all mixed up and misplaced. I looked, and I don't have that napkin with your number anymore."

I looked out to the sun and the ocean, then back to her. How similar her smile was to the sun. Wow, I had been drinking too much.

"I wanted to come over and tell you, Scott, because I remember that first night we talked and how nice you were and how interesting our conversation was. I cannot talk like that with anyone except my best friend, and I just met you. I could have talked to you all night." She smiled again.

I sat back and looked at her. She was a philosopher. Who would have known? She continued, "So write me your number, and I'll call you, and we can try again."

I started daydreaming while listening to her. It is a shame things do not work out as we would dream them. We would dream them up a very nice way to make them work. Dream the whole world. Things seldom work as we dream, but that is no reason not to. I looked up at her and spoke, "OK."

"How about a Belgian white with lemon instead of the Corona? They are great. It's the first time we've had it on tap."

I exhaled deeply, squinting into the sun, then looked at her. I thought of my life and when making money to keep a straight head and not making money to keep a straight heart. I thought about Audrey and then Christina, and looked over at the woman with straight brown hair and the man she was in love with who had the terrible voice, and felt remorse. I was in love, and I thought how strange the consequences of small actions push tiny waves of change through an entire life. I tried to shake the dust off my heart and answer.

"OK sure. Don't worry about the other day," I said, looking at Christina. "Belgian white sounds great." Christina rose and returned to her bar. I watched her leave, took out a napkin, and wrote my number on it and then my name. Christina returned with a tall glass of cold light beer. There was a wedge of lemon stuck to the lip, sitting in the small foamy head. I took it, thanked her, and handed her the napkin with my number. She smiled and said some nice things and returned to her bar. She would call me soon. I took the lemon from the glass and squeezed it over the beer, dropped it in, took the glass up, and had a drink. It was icy cold and very good. I looked at the water. There were two large, white swans swimming together by the dock. I watched them, and then I said it. I did not mean to, but it just came out. I said it before I could catch myself. Damn. Damn. Maybe someday I will be able to go a day without saying it. "I miss Audrey."

I looked around. Two women and a man walked out on the deck beside me. They carried large icy dull red Margaritas that had moisture droplets on the glasses. One of the women turned, and I noticed the smooth roundness of her bottom. It was marvelous and salient as a peach as if carved by Rodin if Rodin would have sculpted with Dungaree. This work of art sat on a chair, facing away from me, the other two sat down with her. They were laughing and drinking. I returned to my drink, let my eyes stray, and watch them but noticed nothing else worth mentioning to you. I took the last bite of casadia, folded the napkins, and placed them in my front left pocket. I was sure I would not say it again that day. I looked over at Christina and smiled then leaned back in the cast white heat of the sun and enjoyed my beer.

ONE JANUARY NIGHT

I drove home with the scents of your house,
The faint taste of lemon tea,
The darkened horizon of your window's view
And stars hid by clouds of snow
And sleeping trees draped with ice,
You and I looking at the night
Cold, snowy, windy, warm,
Your eyes in the darkness soft,
Behind, the ship, the house, twinkling to the sea
With silent bells.
I did not know
What little wells were filling
When I knocked at your door,
Under the tawny white shadows of the trees,
Or how many times the sun would rise
And set under the crackling gray sea ice
Where the joy
And etchings of that stillness,
Like apples on a tree,
Fall to sleeping dreamers
Painting frescos
Of bright springtime orchards
Splashed with stars
Kissing in the wind.

AT THE TAMARACK

The Tamarack was the kind of fast-food restaurant you see near the beach that sells burgers, fries, and fried fish and has the picnic tables and chairs outside. The tables and chairs were old, and there were not even umbrellas.

"How's the food here?" Scott asked.

"It is great," Christina said.

"Have you ever had Kelly's in Revere?"

"It is better than Kelly's in Revere." Christina took Scott's hand and walked with him, away from the car, toward the restaurant.

Scott had grown up eating at Kelly's in Revere, and as far as he was concerned, it was the best; and he did not feel like converting today. He was hungry. It was hot, and in the heat, he felt it more. There was coldness between him and Christina. It was difficult to fake intimacy, but always easier while there was something to do. The distance between them closed a bit as they walked to the Tamarack.

Scott stood and examined the Tamarack's white signs. He noted the sandwiches and dinners, the chowders and specials; and Christina spoke, not to him directly, just aloud, reading the items she thought she might enjoy. Scott was hungry and smelling the food and decided what he would enjoy the most while nodding at her suggestions.

"Do you know what you want, Scotty?" She squeezed his hand. They held hands, but there was a distance between them as there is always between people who make love but do not love each other.

"I think I will have three lobster rolls." He joked.

"Sure, you spend sixty dollars on your lunch." Her face moved toward his, and she planted a kiss.

"When I was a little girl, my father used to take my sisters and me here all the time." She pulled away and smiled.

"Are we in Laconia?"

"Yes." She indicated, pointing to a sign.

"The last time I was in Laconia, I was eight and on my father's friend's boat," Scott said.

"We didn't have a boat," Christina said. "We used to go to Weirs Beach."

"I remember Weirs Beach. They have the water slides?"

"They're about ten minutes away." She pointed in a direction.

"How are the fish plates here?" Scott asked.

"They're so good." Christina reassured.

"I think I will get fish and chips then." He felt her move closer and then her soft mouth on his cheek.

"I am not very hungry," she said. She stood silent and read the menu. Scott enjoyed the momentary silence. He looked and saw a fat orange sign across the street along the road that read, Caution! Construction! "¡Construcción! ¡Precaución!"

Scott watched as a portly yellow bulldozer dragged a lumpish tree across the ground. There were men standing around in yellow hard hats pulling at the trees with steel chains. They were clearing a large section of land for a new building's construction.

"Why don't you get lobster?" Scott asked Christina. Christina was softly singing a song and dancing with her hips.

"I want clams."

Christina took his other hand while she danced and sang, and Scott smiled and silently castigated himself. What a fool. After all this time, still cannot forget and imagine she is *the one, the one who got away*, standing with him. Scott looked at Christina. She was holding his hand, beautiful, enchanting. The yellow sun was high and a delight, and the ride had been very pleasant and enjoyable in his new convertible. He had been making money at writing and felt grand. He nodded as Christina spoke, pretending to listen while scrutinizing her. She looked nothing like *her*. He closed his eyes to disperse the memories.

Christina was real. She was beautiful with her delicate face and magnificent head of straight blond hair. She smiled with two dimples that on a man would have made him look like Tony Curtis. Her forehead and her chin were distinguished, and one would remember those first after the dimples and blond hair, if it were not for the eyes. Her eyes were like golden blue pools surrounded by white sands. They were exciting, friendly, always open, and happy, with happy things in them. They invited you in and told you there were happy fun things to do and happy fun excitement to be had and in their own magic conveyed absolutely that she was on your side. To Scott, they had been the bait that drew him to her, but what caught him was her mouth. It was full and smiling, and as he got to know her, it became a frightening object of desire.

"I'm having either a clam plate or clam boat," Christina said.

"All right."

They walked up to the counter.

Behind the white Tamarack counter, a woman, tired and gray, greeted them. She looked like a peasant woman out of a Steve McCurry photograph. Next to her stood a young woman of high school age dressed in yellow. The old woman was instructing her.

"First, you take their order."

The high school girl's eyes focused on Scott, and the woman flushed and spoke, "Can I help you?"

Scott motioned. Christina moved next to him, holding his hand. "I will have the clam boat with french fries and coleslaw."

"I'll have the fish and chips." Scott finished.

"One clam boat with fries and slaw and one fish and chips." The peasant woman repeated, showing the girl in yellow where to punch the register.

"Now their drinks." The old woman indicated.

"I'll have spring water," Scott said.

"Do you have iced tea? I'll have an iced tea," Christina spoke. Scott reached into his pocket and took out a fold of money.

The old woman smiled and flushed, looking very hot in the heat. She pointed to the young girl.

"I am teaching her today. This is my youngest daughter."

"That's great!" Christina crinkled her blue eyes. "You're doing great."

"Thank you." The high school girl smiled. "You are number 37." She handed Christina the receipt.

The day was sunny and blue with very little wind but much heat. Scott examined and read the orange Tamarack signs.

"Lobster roll sales record: 887 sold in one day." He pointed the sign to Christina who had begun reading also. Much of it consisted of "did you know?" and every one was about the Tamarack.

"Did you know we use enough hot dog buns to line the Fleet Center floor three and a half times?"

"Did you know our lobster rolls are 100 percent lobster-langoustine meat?"

"What is langoustine?" Scott asked Christina.

"It's like a crawfish, we used to play with them in the water behind my house." She kissed him.

"The lobster rolls are made from langoustine and lobster meat." He pointed to a sign.

A pair of motorcycles bellowed and rolled into the Tamarack parking lot. They were Harley-Davidsons—one black Road King Classic with a black-and-chrome twin-cam engine, and the other, maroon Sportster with a chrome-staggered exhaust. Their metal glistening in the sun, the two riders disembarked then walked up to order. Christina examined the Road King Classic.

"It is very nice." Her blue eyes strained in the yellow sun.

"My friend Beto works for Harley-Davidson," Scott said, looking at the bikes.

"Really?" Christina's blue eyes smiled wistfully.

"Yes. He can tell the different types of Harleys by the sound of their exhaust."

"Who is that?"

"Beto. You remember him? You met him when we were in the Copley Square."

"Oh yeah."

"He says it is something in the way a Harley swallows and ejects air." Scott tried to make the noise with his throat but failed.

Another motorcycle, this one very loud too, pulled up. There was a pepper-haired man driving with a woman seated behind him. The bike was also a Harley. Scott guessed it was an Electra Glide. The couple dismounted. Both had long hair under their helmets, and their hair went wild as they removed them. They walked up to the Tamarack to order. As they ordered, seven or eight more motorcycles bellowed past the Tamarack.

"It must be Bike Week." Scott watched them pass.

"Next week," Christina told him. As she spoke, she noticed an older couple eating at one of the picnic tables on the shaded side of the restaurant. They sat close, eating quietly under the green trees. Christina watched, her blue eyes soft with sentiment. Apparently, their age was an example of lasting love.

"Aren't they adorable?" Scott did not remark but watched the tall, grizzled owner of the Road King carry lobster rolls over to the picnic tables under the trees' shade and sat down to eat.

"Number 37," an electronically modulated voice spoke. Christina walked over and picked up the orange tray, and Scott picked up the spring water and the iced tea and asked the old lady behind the white counter, "What is langoustine?"

"It is a type of crawfish," the peasant woman explained.

"Thank you."

Christina filled up the tray with ketchup, napkins, straws, and tartar sauce. "Where would you like to sit, Scotty?" She looked at the green picnic tables under the trees, at the white ones behind the Tamarack in the sun, and at the large red-and-white screen house up the hill.

She was finished loading the tray.

"Wherever is fine." He looked at her blue eyes.

"Let's eat in the sun," she said.

They walked together up to the white picnic tables behind the Tamarack in the sun, over the clean green earth, and sat down.

"Don't you just love summer?" she spoke, smiling with her eyes.

"Langoustine is crawfish," Scott said, sitting down.

"I know. We used to play with them when I was a kid."

"I bet that is why the lobster rolls are so cheap here. At Kelly's in Revere, they are expensive." He looked back at the building.

"Mmmmm. So yummy."

"I didn't think you ate fried food," he said.

"I usually don't, but I love it."

Scott ate.

"It's good."

He ate quickly, as it is easy to do with fried food—opening a tartar sauce, dipping pieces of fish, lifting a few french fries, stabbing them into the ketchup, then biting them, and repeating. He ate his while it was hot, holding his fork for the coleslaw and, every now and then, tasting it. He watched Christina feeling closer to her and thought, maybe it was the pleasure of the food. He watched her open a small-side container of clear liquid, dip a french-fried potato into it, and then eat it.

"What is that?" he asked.

"Vinegar." She handed it to him.

"Really?"

"Have you ever tried it?" Christina smiled, showing her white teeth.

"No."

"It's very good. Try some." She slid it closer.

"All right." He dipped a french fry in and tasted it.

"It's OK." He had tried it, he remembered, in a memory far, far back. It was with Audrey visiting her family in the Vineyard, some time back. Scott closed his eyes and chewed to chase away the memories.

"This is the wrong kind of vinegar. It should be the dark malt vinegar." Christina left the small cup between them.

"Vinegar on french fries?"

For a long time, there was only the touch of the breeze in the leaves and the sound of their own eating. The food got cold very quickly. Silences are never awkward when alone, and sometimes we find others with whom we can be silent with and enjoy. But after some time, this silence became difficult and very apparent, and the food no longer helped.

"What is wrong, Scotty?" Christina's red mouth and blue eyes converged.

"Nothing," he said. He looked at her. For a moment, she flared before him like the sun then waned and became a simple face.

"You have been like this all morning."

"It's nothing," Scott said.

"Is there anything I can do?" She touched his hand.

"No."

"You know, when I was living in Laconia, I used to come here all the time with my sister." Her blue eyes hovered as wisps under the gold-pink-yellow sun.

"Which sister?" He watched.

"The one that is a geneticist."

"The same that you are going to see the River Dancers with on Saturday?"

"Yes. Though all my sisters are going."

They sat silent for a moment.

"Do you enjoy being the middle sister?" Scott asked.

"I do, but sometimes I wish I were the youngest. My younger sister has it so easy." Her blue eyes blinked gray then silver.

"The eldest put your parents through it all already." Scott joked.

"I was a good girl." She sparkled.

"And now look at you."

"Yeah. Can you even stand to sit with me?"

"No. You are corrupting me."

"I've always been wild. I'm trying to push you over the edge."

"Wild is what I need. But it'll be your fault if I become a freak," he joked. She laughed.

"You are a freak!"

Scott was silent. He watched the pepper-haired biker, smoking and talking to the woman he rode in with. She was finishing an ice cream.

"Scotty." Christina kissed his cheek.

"Yeah?"

"You are not worried about this morning, are you?"

"This morning?"

"Don't be."

He smirked. She spoke, "I wanted it to happen."

"Me too."

"You did?" She screwed her neck and sat back.

"Yes. That's how I want you, barefoot and at home so I can go chase college girls." He laughed.

"I cannot talk to you." She moved away.

A Tamarack employee walked by, shaking out a black trash bag. He was changing the bins in the parking lot. Another employee opened the back door and shouted something, and then both returned inside.

"Scotty, don't be worried." Her blue eyes flashed.

"I won't." He looked at her.

"Don't." Her eyes commanded.

"I wish I had not done it." He looked away.

"I loved it. I felt so close to you." Her voice soothed.

"But I wish I had not."

"Don't worry." She reassured with her eyes.

"I'm not."

"I just love when you do that."

He looked at her.

"Blame me," she said. "I asked you to." Her eyes sighed blue in the golden sun.

"No. I did it."

She looked at him.

"It's hard to think during," she said, her eyes filling. "I get so lost and excited."

"I couldn't think either." Scott spoke, watching her.

"I love it," she said.

Scott looked toward the orange construction signs.

"Scotty, don't worry." She moved toward him and kissed his cheek.

"I'm not. If anything it is biology that worries me, that's all. Mother nature."

"Only once." She reassured.

"That's all you need."

"Don't be a freak." She sat back and ate a french fry dipped in vinegar.

"I'm not."

"I want to make you happy."

"You do." Scott reassured her.

"You would make a great father, but I don't want a baby."

From the road, a blue SUV pulled into the parking lot. A woman with yellow hair stepped out. She unhooked her child's car seat and helped a small blond boy in a blue sailor suit step down. The woman held the child's hand. She was talking on a cell phone.

"That SUV is very nice."

"It's a Cadillac I think," Scott said.

"It is very nice." She watched.

"I don't like SUVs."

"I would like one for the winter." White snow fell in the blue of her eyes.

"I watched a TV show about SUVs," Scott spoke from a memory. "*Frontline*. Have you seen it? SUVs are dangerous."

"How?" Her eyes shook the snow into a storm.

"They are prone to roll over."

"I would buy the safest one." Her eyes were an icy blizzard.

"Have you ever watched *Frontline*?"

"No." The snows settled.

"I watched this great show your sister would like on transgenic transplants."

"Really?"

"Yes. Geneticists grow modified animal organs for transplant recipients." Scott sipped a drink of water.

"I am an organ donor, you know." Christina's blue eyes chewed the baby blue.

"Are you?"

"Yes. They will dissect me when I die."

"And they'll scream when they see you're a funky green alien." They both laughed.

"They will." He continued. "Then aliens will come back, get your brain, and leave your green blood to science."

"You can forget a ride in my spaceship." She stuck her pink tongue out.

Scott smiled. Christina sat back but returned.

"What are you thinking?"

"I was just watching that construction site over there. Watching the trees. I think they are ripping them all down. Even the tall, old ones."

"I know. Isn't that sad? Probably for a mall or condo."

Scott watched the construction site. He unconsciously felt the rabbit's foot in his pocket, shriveled and hard, the hair long worn off. He was thinking about the starfish Audrey had given him all those years before at the beach, and how most of the starfish's points had broken off, and how brittle it was. And because of that, he couldn't carry it anymore.

"Scotty." Christina's blue eyes popped and snapped. "Are you finished?" She stood.

"I am."

"Scott, don't worry about this morning. It is only one time. We usually have something. We'll get something for the next time." She carried the orange tray to the trash bin. Across the street, there was a noise of engines and chains and the grinding of gears.

"I know," Scott said. He closed his eyes and let out a deep breath, and his mind idled in a place of great pain as he remembered. No amount of progress or building uproots the deepest things. He pushed the memories away, opened his eyes, and stood. "Let's go to the Weirs. I'd like to see them."

"The water slides?" Christina's pink lips smiled.

"Yeah, the water slides."

THE LADY WITH THE DOG

While my dog, Summer, was alive,
I took dinner by the garden and was happy.
You came home from work and kissed my lips.
You walked barefoot on the beach and held my hand,
And we visited seashell beaches in Falmouth
Whispering in the night on blankets.

In March, I told you I was unsure,
I was not ready to be in love,
Sitting with my neighbors, I shook my head,
That old pain inside, beating, shuddering.

In July, I kissed you first.
Standing by the train to say good-bye.
You, such a charmer always, blushed.
That smile forever changed me inside out.

In November, I took your key,
And ordered you never to come back, the rain driving cold.
I cried and cried and cried.
The days grew short, and my neighbors moved away.

You apologized a hundred times.
I claimed to know everything about my heart.
I said I was too old for this type of pain
And never wanted that again.
The green leaves—brown with winter,
The garden abandoned to the cold.
It is lonely at night.
I light candles and see things
In the flames that make me cry.
Summer died some time ago and is gone, buried
In the corner of the garden.

THE DOORS ON THE STREET

Sometimes when you wake, the morning is much different than you can believe, and your head does not hurt from drinking or staying up late, nor do you feel bad really except for your conscience. You wake and look to see if it is true, and it is, so you repent and get out of bed. You must be quiet. You do not want to disturb anything. If only you could disturb everything and, like a holiday ball, shake it and watch new snow cover everything. You look at the bed, and then wish you had not looked and again repent. If only you were stronger. You could have said anything. Anything like the standard excuses: it's not you it's me. I'm not ready for a commitment. I think you're really fun but there's no future here. Rock and roll needs a new king, and you're leaving for Las Vegas. You try to remember why you did not, and then you remember and feel a bit foul and repent even more. At this rate, you will be ordained.

In the shower, you wash and feel the hot water, going over each spot twice to get clean, three times for some spots. And after, in front of the mirror, you brush your teeth and even floss; but the soap did not remove it, and you gargle and spit in the sink. You rinsed the best you could. Maybe it will help to clean your ears. Yes. Dante wrote of wax. We must remove it all. And then there is the sun through the window. You look and look away. Maybe some deodorant and fresh clothes. The sun beats not there, despite its light, hot on the floor.

You walk silently into the kitchen. Maybe a glass of water, some orange juice, a hot cup of black coffee, or green Sencha tea, waffles with melted butter, maple syrup, and the butter melted in the grooves. Maybe some bacon, sizzling. Life is always easier while eating. Maybe scrambled eggs, more coffee, ketchup, Tabasco for the eggs, and a pad more of butter for the waffles with syrup, salty and sweet.

The coffee is very hot, and maybe that will do the trick. Maybe if you put on your watch and shoes and check your pockets to see that you have everything, and then take a walk, remembering to keep to the plans you made while eating.

Maybe if you run an errand or do that bit of work you have been putting off. You even consider things you have put off for a long while, and do not like doing if it will help. You might wash that part behind your ears or the dishes or even do the laundry. Maybe your reform will go fabulously, and you will leave the situation atoned, making a new life somewhere else.

You feel the lightness of anxiety that lifts you from under the feet. Swallow the coffee. Try a deep breath. You have done it this time. It will be all right. It is always all right. Why be so hard? You begin to act patient, trying to understand and believe it will be, and that this is the way of things. You take the pot of coffee and pour another cup. You will finish your breakfast and then leave.

You do not need anyone else to do these things. You swallow down the coffee. It is hot and pungent and lifts your blood. You swallow the strong roasted taste while shutting off the machine, snapping the filter and pouring the grounds in the trash. It makes too much noise. You do not want to make noise! Damn! Stupid fool. Do not be loud! Damn! I can be loud. I should be loud. Be quiet, who has transgressed. You, sinner. Forgive me for I sinned. Now stop talking to yourself.

You stand by the door, holding your breath to be silent. Maybe it would go better if you explained it like it is, telling how you really hate being alone and are a terrible person, and it was a moment of weakness because it is lonely and difficult to be alone in the night. It is difficult, and it is human; but it is neither difficult nor human to lie. You think of the night, of how big it is and how difficult it is to tell the truth in it. You do not enjoy lying and feel terribly that you have, and they must understand it is not what you really wanted to do. You do care for them, even though they don't care, they must understand that you feel different and have different wants and dreams and could not possibly be happy if you stayed.

Maybe you could blame your job, say the business is taking you away and you need to gather your head and will be out of town. Maybe you could blame alcohol and its quirks, lose yourself in it, and forget it all. Maybe you could say it is another lover, that they love you for who you really are and you are going back to them; and therefore, it would be impossible, or maybe you could tell the truth. No. No. It is too late for truth.

You wonder if the neighbors will question. They are so inquisitive. Busybodies have nothing better to do. The night is dark and easy to hide in, and no one would ever turn on your lights. You must do something because if you do not, you will be in a situation that is unacceptable, and you cannot have that because you are above these things. They must understand and be civil and honor you and be forthcoming and serious and not misunderstand.

You promise yourself never again and reprimand yourself with a hundred moral phrases. You should know better. What were you thinking? What would your mother think? It was all wrong and stupid, lead me not into temptation, especially in the night when I am alone and it is dark and the night is long and lonely. Why is the night so long? Perhaps it is God's first joke.

You remember details of being loved by someone you truly cared for, and when that ended, you promised you would get that love back. But these things take time and a good deal of luck. Dr. Pangloss was right. This is the best of all possible worlds, and just as the palate was made to enjoy coffee, so there is coffee and the right foot was made to press an accelerator, and therefore, we have cars. The heart was made to long in the dark, and therefore, we have lies.

You remember the details of last night, and shrug and feel stupid and lost. No, not lost. No. Not ever. Not lost. To hell with being lost. I am still here. I am alive. I am not like those people. I will never be like those people who use themselves as much as others use a drink or a drug. I am special, different, and only lonely; and I had been for a very long time and was due. It is very lonely, and you were due for a victory. You are better than most because you are good, and when you die, it is all over. You are not a priest or lawyer or doctor, you are just a human being who is trying, and you deserve the best. In the book of Job, Job lost everything but was restored. Odysseus suffered too, and so will you. You will because we all must. You are sick of all the dust.

But if we are dust, none of that matters. Glaukos was right; we are like leaves upon the earth, cast to the ground by wind. Maybe we all turn to dust, and all is lost. Ten thousand generations of man upon this earth, and yet we still act as rats in alleys, picking dead men's bones, killing each other over greed. I do not want to turn to dust. Maybe dust is not so bad. Turn. Take your share and turn. Turn and walk the earth. But beware those who walk up and down, to and fro. Instead, walk east to west, picking bones before yours are stripped. Absolutely. We are rats in alleys where dead men lose their bones.

You absolutely must get out of here!

Maybe if you escape, you can become another person. No. Madam Fate would never allow it. She has dealt the cards. She would close her black umbrella with a smile and offer an aperitif. And I would say, "Please let me be an old and dusty tree. Or a fish in silver mail, gliding in the deep; or a bird in the sky, flying toward the sun! Just set me free!" If only I could be because I am. You want to be, yet are eternally. So you must leave. Get away. Go away and go west like a prospector and search for buried gold. Buried gold bullion. Where was El Dorado? I shall shake forty sheep from the earth, find an island, and be done! Like Robinson Crusoe, planting my days' ideas for tomorrow. Saving my rum. Loving God. But where are the sheep to carry all this gold? Poseidon drowned them. Aphrodite scorned. Even the king, the father, mighty Zeus, destroyed the air.

I shall need help. Who is left? Great Hera! Wise Athena! Noble Apollo! Watch the crowds, they throw the old gods from London Bridge. Where are the friends and lovers, dinners and parties, care and loving making, and that feeling that nothing has been missed? Trapped in still pictures? Black-and-white prints of silver gelatin tacked to refrigerators and glass frames? Sun tea brewing in the window, conversations in the hall, flags on the ramparts? Gelatin prints etched silver in time with family and friends, lovers and loves lost, covered with dust from restless nights in one-night cheap hotels, sawdust restaurants, and oyster shells. While all the trees—dusted, ripped up, and torn, removed forever from the earth—are replaced with the Works. Nothing will be left but ghosts, malls, silence, condominiums, and steel barbed wire around it all. The corpses of a million dead cars. The old rusted pipes of the latrines. The twisted steel beams of the metropolis.

Each day is art, and each night contains a year's worth of pain. I do not know if there is any trust for hope. Does anyone care? Perhaps the Muses are the only ones capable of saving us. War and peace are arts, after all. And it is in art that life is fair, and love is perfect.

Oh bravo! You are so kindhearted! So kind!

Blood and love as art! A bloody genius you are. A bloody Russian constructivist! Memories are all that live! Edit them together! Look, it's Eisenstein incarnate! Or would it be Bazin? Memory is night with fog—you can't see anything, and even with light, it is just a blur. There were no doomsday weapons hidden in Arabia, just a thousand and one bloody nights for the young to die. Where are the clairvoyants? Burned all their tarot cards and came down with the flu. Madam Sosostris has been missing too. The dead stink up the land, and the land becomes a waste. I put on cologne and smell better than my neighbors and my enemies, but even they have someone to hold them in the night.

Hold your breath! Listen! You don't need primping! You have been too loud! Hope you were not heard! Stop breathing! Keep still as a cat! Listen and dread, and you cannot stay still and remain. You must flee! But the sun is up! The day is beautiful, and the mockingbird is on the roof. He is singing his song. Wonder how long he'll sing today? That voice is chameleon. He has been out there for a week, all through the Fiesta de San Pedro. He sings his love song, calling to his *amoure*, yet she has not come. Where is she? It is humid and hot, and he sings for her. He sings his song and jumps, throwing himself straight up in the air, his tail flopping over his head like a ribbon trailing from a child's kite only to land on his wiry feet, and starts his calling dance all over again. The inexplicable splendor of the bird's green and gold. *Darling! Darling love! Wild bird! Where are you flying? I am still here! Singing! I sing for you! Hear me! Love! I sing! I sing every day! I sing and dance for you!*

> Fate had her way. The madam smiles. I am sure.
> The tower has been hit by lightning and is aflame.
> The moment of dread becomes a womb of no escape. Please! No! I am dust.

And then a noise, a stir and a stretch, a yawn and a roll, slowly, ever so. And then the crumpling of the sheets, a rising hair bent, squiggled, and matted from sleep then a rubbing of eyes. They blink, and finding you, they smile. And you are struck a stupid fool.

"Hello love," a voice says.

"Good morning."

"Can you believe it, love?"

"What's that?"

"This, love, our first morning as husband and wife."

A LULLABY TO VANITY

> What do people gain from all
> >the toil
> >at which they toil under the
> >sun?
> A generation goes, and a
> >generation comes,
> >but the earth remains forever.
>
> —Ecclesiastes 1:3-4

In a New England country store in 1910, a group
of worn old men in dark clothes sat near a wood-
burning stove, playing chess. Smoking their
tobacco pipes,

Queen!

    King!

Knight!

I sat and watched,
The statues black-and-white.
Those wrinkled chaps with bluing faces sucked on pipes,
The smoke rose through the luster of the lights.

Many people came and went,
Buying ice and tea and peppermint.

Working class: suspenders, caps, overalls.
Many, many, many licked the dust from the corners of their mouths,
Removed their hats, and wiped the sweat from off their brows.
Labor, work, and always more;
Rolling on its back, a tired dog upon the floor.
Running, lifting, dropping, breathing, crying—
While Aaron Copland kindly trying . . .

Gelatin Silver Print

It was the year of the economic fall
And ice, we skied until the night
Had blued amid the trees and laughed our
Breath to steam.

Still,
Many people came and went,
Buying ice and tea and peppermint.

Family love is all we need
With us in our bit of life;
With us in our life of work;
With us as we curl at the end of dusk with empty plate and paper dust and stand beside their bosoms thus and proudly say, "This is me. This is what I have done! This has been my thrust!"

A bit of hope, a bit of sun,
To fetch a smile, light a room,
To bring us as we slip and fall, a bit of mint and ice and kisses after all.

I have seen the restless rolling of the days,
Seen them all the same, all the same,
Yet day to day, we dare the game:

Queen!

    King!

Knight!

I have been a chess piece checked between
So many pieces that
I have fallen flat upon my back,
Pausing, bruised, while looking back,
To hide my face that's brightly rouged.

Check! Check! Checkmate!
I have heard eternal voices snicker,
I have heard bangs end with but a whimper.

Tired hands, proudly holding still
While in our time, we grieve loves ground up in the mill.

I work, I work, I work,
I work as I have told;
I worked so many days I missed my growing old,
And like a cat, I have curled and lay in corners cold.
Tomorrow I will rise to meet the day again,
Greet the day and strain and, in so, make my shoulders pain.
My back, the land, my hands, the sea,
My eyes,
The sky,
Ache mortality.

There upon that distant sky, we pray and listen,
Pray and wait,
Waiting for the sun and stars to fall burning on our plate.
Yet in the rain I cry and listen to the singers singing by,
Because I too sing:

I sing for hope, I sing with ease,
I sing in cellar restaurants and streets,
I sing on shiny holidays with trees,
I sing with muddy hands,
I sing with powdered feet,
I sing with bits of shellfish in my teeth,
With whistles in my nose, a muffled rag doll in my clothes,
I sing because I love!

And with my mortal jaw too
Grab and hold the ocean by the claw,

I love!

But everything fades,
Even vanity.
And now my bit of love, my song of life, is but a child's voice,
At night.
Yet somehow,
Somehow,
That seems right.

Made in the USA
Lexington, KY
07 September 2011